A BARGAIN to KEEP

ALENA MENTINK

ELECTRIC
MOON
PUBLISHING

ELECTRIC
MOON
PUBLISHING

www.emoonpublishing.com

DEDICATION

For Kailey—you earned it

A man's heart deviseth his way:
But the Lord directeth his steps.
—Proverbs 16:9 KJV

1

Columbus, Nebraska
July 31, 1878

The nice saying that time made everything better was a lie.

Jeanne dunked a plate into her rinse water, then piled it to dry with about twenty others. And the stack of used plates still towered. She hadn't known an establishment could own so many plates until she had come to work at the Columbus Hotel, but she now stood corrected. She could wash dishes all morning and still not be caught up by lunchtime.

Jeanne heaved a sigh and plunged her hands into the dishwater again, fingers seeking the next plate. One week working for the hotel and already she felt trapped, smothered by the effort of trying to fit in with the staff and keep up with the work. They needed more help—everyone knew it—but Mr. Greason seemed uninclined to do anything to remedy the situation. He probably figured hiring Jeanne had been enough.

The others seemed to think it would have been—if Jeanne would run a little faster, cut her words with customers to a bare minimum, and above all, learn to keep her stomach from rebelling at inconvenient moments.

No, time didn't make everything better. Just three weeks ago, her biggest concern had been getting Irving's supper on the table at six o'clock sharp, and now she was praying for the strength just to make it through one more miserable day—one more day of enduring the blistering heat of the kitchen, one more day of keeping Mr. Greason happy with her efficiency, one more day of tolerating all the hotel's nasty smells that only heightened her morning sickness. And the worst thing was that she could see no end to this misery.

"Jeanne!" Effie Harding flew through the door that separated the kitchen from the dining room. "Would you get out here and help? I've got crowds of diners waiting for their orders to be filled, and you're working on the *dishes?* Can't you use your head to see what needs to be done?"

Use your head. Jeanne's face heated, and wiping her hands on her apron, she hurried toward Effie. "I'm sorry."

She nearly collided with Cook, and as Cook began spluttering, Jeanne mumbled another apology and ducked around her.

Everything would have been simple if Irving hadn't up and died. Actually, everything would have been simple if she had never married Irving in the first place. If Papa hadn't been so certain that women's minds were too weak to grasp the concept of money, he wouldn't have forced her and Irving to marry over his deathbed, and if she hadn't married Irving, Papa's inheritance would still be safely in the bank, not lost at the gaming tables.

That wasn't to say that Irving hadn't been a good man. He did his duty and made sure the larder was full, and he was smart enough that he never gambled them into debt—just the next thing to it.

But that didn't mean she had loved him.

Jeanne pushed the dining room door open, shaking her head to dispel the thought of Irving. She had been thinking of him more in the past couple days, trying to remember what color his eyes had been and wondering what color his hair had been before he lost it, which had been long before she was introduced to him. She had never found the right moment to tell him about the baby on the way.

Jeanne scanned the dining room, searching for the most impatient-looking customer, and saw the Columbus sheriff seated by the window. There. He was the one she would target. It would never do to make the sheriff impatient.

Even Effie can't fault that logic.

Sheriff Calaman and his friend were busy looking at a bunch of paper spread on the table before them, and Jeanne stopped beside their table, clearing her throat. Neither of the men looked up.

Jeanne shifted from one foot to the other, and since the sheriff's friend was seated closer to her, she tapped him on the shoulder. "Excuse me!"

He spun around so fast that the brim of his hat hit her arm and sent his hat tumbling. "Do you have to scare a man like that?"

Oh, dear—now she had made him mad. Why was she always sticking her wrong foot forward?

"I'm sorry." Jeanne smiled, trying to smooth the situation over, but he didn't smile back. Jeanne bit her lip. Well, she would just have to show him that she meant no harm. Jeanne bent to pick up his hat, and too late, saw that the man had the same idea. Their heads connected with a crack. He yelped, and she staggered back, a blur of colors swirling in her vision. That definitely had *not* been the way to win herself into his good graces.

Shaking her head to clear it, Jeanne fumbled for the notebook in her pocket and turned to Sheriff Calaman. She had no hope of getting anywhere with his friend. "Your order?"

The sheriff didn't seem impressed with her performance. "Roast dinner and potatoes and gravy, if you will. And apple cobbler for dessert."

She nodded and scribbled the note down, then made herself face the sheriff's friend again.

He didn't look particularly impressed either. "Same as Calaman," he said, lifting a hand to rub his forehead. Jeanne's eye caught on a metallic glint on his shirt. Oh, dear. So he was a lawman too.

"I'll bring your order shortly," she said, spinning away on her heel. *Jeanne McAllister, if you don't get this job straightened out, Mr. Greason is going to fire you, and then you'll be in a real mess.*

Jeanne shoved through the door to the kitchen, a blast of heat hitting her in the face. Would getting fired really be so bad? On a July day like this when the mercury was in the nineties, working in the kitchen was brutal.

But she needed this job. The position had come as a direct answer to prayer, and with that being the case, she really had no right to complain.

Jeanne grabbed two plates and set to work dishing them up with man-sized helpings. Effie stuck her head through the door and yelled for three more plates, so Jeanne dished up those as well, then arranged the dishes on two serving trays. Hoisting one on each hand, she shoved the door open with her hip and made her way into the dining room.

"Over here, Jeanne!" A blond at a nearby table waved her down, then began inspecting her immaculate hand as Jeanne shifted directions and walked toward her.

"Miss Maynard, I hope you're doing well." Jeanne knew her voice sounded strained, but Allison Maynard could ruin a day just by showing her face.

"Oh, Jeanne, it's just *Allison*." Allison smoothed down her full skirts, the little smile on her facing telling Jeanne plainly that she knew she was stepping on her nerves. "You've been working here for six days, haven't you?"

Jeanne jerked her head in a nod. And Allison had made sure to make an appearance every one of those days.

"And twenty-one days since your husband died." Allison clucked her tongue. "Such a shame. You were the belle of the ball when you and your father arrived here in Columbus. Guess you should have had the sense to choose a young man before your father married you off to a man not a day younger than himself."

"I'm still glad I turned down your brother's proposal, if that's what you're digging for. And Irving wasn't such a bad man."

Allison's eyebrows rose delicately. "But he gambled you out of your home. How can you call that good?"

"I didn't say that." Jeanne's voice rose a bit higher, and realizing that heads were turning her way, she lowered her voice. "He provided well enough for me while he was alive."

"But now that he's gone, look at where you are. So tragic that you should fall so low!" Allison twisted the ring on her finger, watching Jeanne's face. "Oh, did I forget to mention that I'm engaged? The wedding will be in two months. Not that you'll be there, of course. I'm only inviting the elite, and since you've fallen to this level—well, I'm sure you understand."

Jeanne's face heated. "Allison, why are you rubbing Irving's death in? I know you're angry that I turned down your brother, but it wasn't my fault that he decided to join up with the navy. I'd appreciate if you just left me alone."

Allison pasted on a smile. "Oh, but you shouldn't be alone during this time. Besides, I don't come here to see you. I come for lunch, and if I happen to see you—well, it would be impolite to ignore you."

"I wish you would."

"I have to keep checking on you. I would hate to lose track of you if you were to suddenly lose your job or some such crazy thing."

"Lose my job?" Jeanne stepped closer to her. "What are you talking about?"

"Well, it must be hard for you to be thrust into such a demanding position. And if you're struggling to keep customers happy, why should Mr. Greason keep you on?" Allison waved her hand toward Effie, and Jeanne caught the glare the maid sent her. "I mean, here you are wasting even more time talking to me."

Heat flooded Jeanne's face. "Are you *trying* to see me fail? Is that what you want?" Her voice pitched high again, but Jeanne felt too upset to care. "Maybe this is some kind of a game for you, but I'll have you know that I need this job, and if you try to interfere, you'll be very sorry, Miss Maynard."

Allison pressed a hand to her throat. "Is that a threat?"

"Yes, it is a threat!" Jeanne leaned closer. "And I will act upon it if I need to."

She turned to storm away but stopped short at the sight of a man with a badge blocking her path.

"Now, now—what's the trouble, ladies?" Sheriff Calaman asked, hands on his hips.

The sudden stop shifted all the plates on the trays in Jeanne's hands, and she spread her fingers, desperately trying to regain control. The tray in her right hand began to tip, and Jeanne lunged a step forward in an effort to keep it from spilling. She was too late. The tray full of three plates of roast dinner and potatoes and gravy flipped out of her hands and smacked right into Sheriff Calaman's chest.

Sheriff Calaman uttered the strangest noise Jeanne had ever heard, and Jeanne sucked in her breath. "Sheriff Calaman, I— I'm so sorry!"

His mouth opened and closed, but when no words came out, Jeanne decided it might be best if she fetched a towel for the mess instead. Clutching the remaining tray with both hands, she spun around and crashed right into the second lawman. The tray hit his chest, and before Jeanne had time to blink, his shirt was covered in dinner as well.

"Oh, my! I'm so—"

He grabbed her arms and had them behind her back before the apology was off her tongue.

"Assaulting a law officer is a crime worthy of jail time, you know." His voice was low, but it sent shivers down Jeanne's spine.

"But I didn't mean—it was an accident." Jeanne looked at Sheriff Calaman, willing him to step in and tell his friend to let her go. But the sheriff was looking at Allison instead.

"Was it true that this young woman was threatening you?"

Allison lifted tear-filled eyes. "Yes, Sheriff. She was."

The man holding her arms tightened his grip just a bit, and Sheriff Calaman turned to her, his gaze heavy enough that Jeanne felt the weight straight through her middle. "You, young lady, are in trouble."

2

Sitting in a wooden chair, his arms folded across his chest and his face purposefully blank, Ethan knew the pretty young lady he and Calaman had arrested must think he was heartless—either that or incapable of emotion. She had long ago given up on sending him pleading looks and instead sat slumped in her seat, staring at the judge.

Ethan sneaked a glance at her now, and despite his intentions to keep himself detached from this situation, the misery on her face made him feel a little miserable himself. Now that she wasn't flinging around platters of roast dinner, she really looked quite innocent. A few years younger than him, he guessed, and pretty too. The little glints of red and gold in her brown hair added life to her face. And she had nice eyes as well.

It was just a pity she had such a nasty temper.

Ethan stared down at the floorboards, mentally calculating how much time this court trial was going to add to the rest of the work he needed to get done before he could leave Columbus and get back to Osceola. He had already been gone for two days, and the time was wearing on him. He wanted to sleep in his own bed again, and although he wasn't usually too concerned about his house, the remembrance of the mess he had left in his kitchen bothered him. He hoped none of his neighbors would feel the need to stop by while he was gone.

But most of all, he wanted to see his daughter again. At just two, Vivian seemed to develop more every day, and every day he was away from his little girl left him feeling that he was missing out.

He couldn't wait to get home.

"Ethan!" Calaman's voice cracked across the room, snapping Ethan out of his daydream. He realized that everyone was staring at him, and he straightened in his seat. What had he missed?

"I want to hear your version of the story," Judge Pratt said, motioning him forward.

"Oh, yes. Of course." Ethan stood and moved forward, aware that the judge and Sheriff Calaman were exchanging glances. He gritted his teeth. The two old men thought they were being secretive, but he knew exactly what they were thinking. For some reason they had decided his mind wasn't quite the same since his wife's death two years before, and every visit he made to Columbus only seemed to convince them all the more that they were correct.

And they both had their own prescriptions for how they thought he could be "healed"—and he didn't like either of them.

Dutifully, Ethan placed his hand on the Bible and swore himself under oath to tell the truth and nothing but the truth. The little lady was watching him again, and he found it hard to concentrate. He didn't like taking a woman to court any more than she liked being here, but honestly, it was her own fault that she was sitting there. She needn't look at him as if he were her worst enemy. She had chosen to start throwing roast dinner, so now she would have to pay the consequences for that.

And, of course, there would be consequences. She had disturbed the peace, assaulted two lawmen, threatened a young woman, and on top of that, wasted five good meals of roast beef and ruined Ethan's best shirt. He had taken his handkerchief to the worst of the mess, but he could still feel the unpleasant stickiness and smell the tantalizing aroma. She hadn't even given him time to eat lunch.

Just the thought of the havoc she had wreaked on his day made him irritated all over again.

"So Ethan, tell us what you saw," Judge Pratt said, heavy-lidded eyes fixed on him.

Ethan cleared his throat. "Well, sir, Calaman and I were sitting in the dining room at the Columbus Hotel at noon—"

"Skip the details, please." Judge Pratt waved one beefy hand. "Calaman and Miss Maynard already made it clear where you were—as you would have noticed if you were listening."

Ethan bit down on his tongue and gave a short nod. "Well, sir, I heard someone talking in a raised voice, so I turned around to look and saw—um—ah—"

"Jeanne McAllister," Judge Pratt said a little more loudly than necessary.

"Yes—her. She looked rather angry as she spoke with Miss— Miss—"

"Maynard," Judge Pratt said even more loudly.

"Yes—that's it. Well, Calaman and I sort of watched her for a moment, and when she seemed to be growing a bit more agitated, he walked over to confront her, and I circled around behind, just to make sure she wouldn't try to bolt. Next thing I knew, she had hurled a tray of roast dinner at Calaman, so I moved in closer to determine what should be done next, and she spun around and threw the second tray at me. She—"

"Judge Pratt, I object to his verbs!" Jeanne bounded to her feet, finger leveled at Ethan. "He used the verbs *hurled* and *threw*, which make me sound violent. He doesn't know what he's talking about."

"Sit down, Mrs. McAllister. Please sit down." Judge Pratt wiggled his fingers, and just as Ethan began to fear she wasn't going to listen, she dropped back into her chair, eyes shooting sparks at him.

"Please continue, Ethan," Judge Pratt said, turning back to him.

"Miss Maynard said she did indeed feel threatened by—by—"

"Mrs. McAllister."

"Yes, Mrs. McAllister." Ethan felt a trickle of sweat run down his neck. Why was that name so hard to remember? It was easier to think of her as Jeanne. "Anyhow, Calaman and I arrested Mrs. McAllister, and that sums the matter up."

"Hmm." Judge Pratt drummed his fingers on the table. "What do you think, Ethan? What do you believe her motives were?"

Ethan snapped his head up. "Her motives?"

"Yes, her motives. Do you think it was a purposeful assault, as Calaman claims, or was it an accident, as Mrs. McAllister says?"

"Uh—well—" Ethan's gaze wandered toward Jeanne. Her eyes drilled into his, daring him to try to convict her. She didn't look the type to try to take down a lawman—but Ethan had long ago learned that not all perpetrators of the law were ugly or dumb. In the heat of anger, countless people had lost control and acted up in ways that landed them in jail—even people as pretty as this brunette with red-and-gold highlights.

Looking back at Judge Pratt, he nodded firmly. "Yes, sir, I do believe she meant to assault me and Calaman."

"Judge Pratt!" She was on her feet again, face flushed and eyes flashing. "He has no perception of how things are! He can't tell you what I was thinking!"

Judge Pratt studied her evenly. "Mrs. McAllister, your behavior right now isn't to your benefit."

Her mouth opened and closed, and then she dropped back into her seat, hands clenched so tightly that her knuckles whitened.

"Given the information presented, there's only one verdict I can pronounce," Judge Pratt said, eyes fixed on the papers scattered across his desk. "Mrs. Jeanne McAllister, I'm afraid I must charge you guilty. However, given the questionable circumstances, I'll go easy on you. I fine you ten dollars for disturbing the peace."

Ethan watched her face drain of color, and fearing she was going to faint, he moved toward her. Just as fast, the blood came rushing back to her face in overabundance, and Ethan stepped farther away. Might be best to keep well out of her reach for right now. He had already had a couple lessons today in what could happen when she turned feisty.

She raised her hand. "Judge Pratt?"

His eyebrows bushed upwards. "Yes?"

She squirmed a bit on her seat and looked down. "I don't have ten dollars."

"Ah." Somehow Ethan suspected that Judge Pratt wasn't surprised. "Well, never fear, Mrs. McAllister. I'm sure we can come up with a satisfactory solution. I knew your father and late husband, and I've no doubt that you will pay your debt." Judge Pratt banged his gavel on his desk. "Court adjourned."

Jeanne still didn't look as if she felt well at all, and Ethan felt a pang inside him. She needed to pay for what she had done, but he did hope Judge Pratt wouldn't be too hard on her.

He turned to leave, but Judge Pratt's voice stopped him. "Please, Ethan, stay a moment if you would. You too, Calaman."

Ethan looked around the nearly empty room. That left Miss Maynard as the only person allowed to leave. Given the look on her face, she considered it more of a case of being *forced* into leaving.

Still, she rose from her seat with a sniff and swept out of the room, nose lifted in the air.

Judge Pratt cleared his throat. "Mrs. McAllister, you mentioned that you have no money for a fine, and I believe I have a solution. Or rather, Ethan has a solution."

All eyes turned to him, and Ethan's heart began to pound. "Uh, I don't think so, Judge. I sure don't have a solution for this."

"Fiddlesticks." Judge Pratt turned to Jeanne. "Ethan is the Polk County sheriff, and he lost his wife two years ago."

Ethan made a little sound. He didn't like having that old story dragged out, and he didn't see why Pratt was bringing it up now.

"Ethan also has a two-year-old daughter, and he's been in a fix because he needs someone to take care of her while he's gone during the day. If you would travel to Osceola with him and help out for two weeks, we'll consider the fine cleared. Agreed?"

"Now wait—" Ethan began, but Calaman was already speaking.

"Pratt, that's not the best way to help Ethan. We both know that Ethan needs to leave Osceola entirely to get his mind off his grief."

Pratt's eyes narrowed. "No, the best way for him to forget his grief is for him to remarry, and I think Mrs. McAllister will help him to see the benefits of having a woman in his life again."

"No." Calaman folded his arms across his chest. "Placing a woman in his life is only going to make him think of the past."

"No, it will open his eyes to the future."

"No, his heart will be cracked open all over again."

"No, his heart will make the first steps in healing."

"No, Ethan needs—"

"Stop!" Ethan didn't mean to yell, and he felt his face heat as everyone spun to face him. "I can take care of myself. I have been for two years, and I don't need either of you trying to fix my life. My life is just fine."

Pratt and Calaman exchanged another of those weighty glances, and Ethan would have paid money to know exactly what message they were telegraphing to one another.

Evidently it was a lengthy one. Ethan listened to the seconds ticking past on the clock and shifted from one foot to the other. If these two didn't get things straightened out quickly, he was going to leave, with or without the judge's approval. He had things to do, and he wanted them wrapped up by the crack of dawn tomorrow. He was sick of Columbus and all these shenanigans.

At last Calaman eased back with a sigh. "All right, Pratt. Have it your way. I still don't think it's the best way, but we might as well give your theory a try. There's no way to test mine right now, not as long as he's going to act so stubborn."

"Excellent." Judge Pratt beamed, and it wasn't until he again cracked his gavel on the desk that Ethan realized what had just happened.

"Hold up! I didn't agree to this—"

"Oh, hush." Judge Pratt frowned at him. "You're going to agree to this. You'll see."

Ethan opened his mouth to say more but then caught a glimpse of Jeanne's face. Her expression held all the rebellion that he felt, and somehow that made him feel much better. As long as they were united on this, neither of them would be roped into the ridiculous bargain the judge was proposing.

3

Ethan couldn't believe he was doing this. Evidently Jeanne couldn't either, because she had been wordless since Sheriff Calaman and Judge Pratt dumped her off at the livery.

He had been so firm when Judge Pratt delivered his verdict, but half a day of Calaman haunting his footsteps and telling him he was making a big mistake had left him frayed. Added to that was Mr. Greason's visit, telling Jeanne she was fired, and Judge Pratt's insistence that he could think of no other way for Jeanne to repay her debt—Ethan couldn't stand the despair in her eyes. His resolve broke, and he agreed to take her with him.

"Don't worry, Ethan," Judge Pratt had whispered to him. "You don't have to pay her—I'll handle the fine and the cost of renting her horse."

And the old codger thought he was being sneaky.

He hated being backed down—really hated it. He had made sure the little lady knew he wasn't happy about this, and she had done equally well at making sure he knew she wasn't happy either—especially about the rope tying her horse to his.

"You make me feel like a criminal," she told him as they left the livery and started down the street leading out of town.

"If you don't want to feel like a criminal, think twice before you assault a lawman next time," he replied unfeelingly.

She said nothing for a moment, and Ethan glanced back to make sure she hadn't done something crazy like throw herself off the horse.

She was still there, and as their eyes met she smiled sweetly. "Mr. Becker, I'd like to enlighten you if I may."

"Shoot for it."

"There's a word I think you'll find very handy to add to your vocabulary. It's called *accident*. It means 'occurring by chance; unintentional,' and to use it in a sentence—just as an example, understand—you could say, 'When she spilled a tray of lunch across his shirtfront, it was completely by *accident*.'"

"I see." Ethan frowned at her. "Well, Mrs. McAllister, I'd like to share a word with you as well. It's called *honesty*, and used in a sentence, you could say, 'If she would admit that she was very angry and she intended to spill dinner across the lawman's shirtfront, her *honesty* would remain intact.'"

"Ah, I think I understand, but let me see if I have this right." Her eyebrows arched upward. "Would this be a proper use of the word? 'The lawman had no sense of *honesty* when he told the judge that the kitchen maid had assaulted him, when instead, he was the one who had sneaked up behind her and placed himself in the path of the tray she was carrying.'"

Ethan gritted his teeth but sent her a thin smile. "Keep trying, Mrs. McAllister. You're use of the word is less than a product of *honesty*."

She glared at him, but he pretended not to notice and instead faced forward again. They overtook a wagon rumbling out of town, and Ethan guided their horses around the team, calling out a greeting to the farmer and trying to forget the woman behind him. The farmer didn't seem to notice the rope tying Jeanne's horse to Ethan's, and he grinned after them as if he thought they made an awfully cute couple.

Ethan clenched his jaw all the harder. This was bound to be a long ride—and an even longer two weeks that he was stuck with her.

Irving had often said that in poker the first man to lose his composure lost the game. Well, if that law carried into other matters of life, then Jeanne figured she was a goner. The farther they traveled, the more irritated and tired she felt. About the only good thing about this wretched trip was that her stomach had been behaving since she lost her breakfast this morning. She would have been mortified if she had been forced to make Ethan stop so that she could retch on the side of the road.

But even as her mood deteriorated around her, Ethan seemed to grow more cheerful with every mile they put between themselves and Columbus. He pretty much ignored her, which was just fine with her, but she caught snatches of humming from him, and every time they passed a fellow traveler, he called out his hello almost as if it were a song. The fact that he was happy while she was miserable only made her even more furious with him.

She could hardly wait to get away from him by the time they reached the outskirts of Osceola.

"Well, here she is," Ethan said, finally addressing her. "What do you think?"

She let her eyes sweep over the small cluster of frame buildings that formed the town. Rutted dirt roads marked out the square, and if that little house-like structure was supposed to pass as a courthouse, it was pitiful. The jailhouse was just as unimpressive. "I don't like it."

She had hoped her words would irritate him, but he didn't seem ruffled at all. "You'll get used to it," he said comfortably, clicking his horse forward.

Jeanne vowed that she would *not* get used to it or let herself like it. Not since it was Ethan Becker's town.

"Where is your house?" she asked his back.

"Don't live in town," he replied. "My farm is a little less than a mile outside of town."

"A farm?" Her voice must have reflected her shock, because he turned to look at her.

"Ever lived on a farm?" he asked.

She shook her head. "Never."

"Well, guess that explains a lot about you." Stopping in front of one of the stores, he dismounted and tied his horse to the hitching rail, then untied her horse from his and tied it to the rail as well. Jeanne watched his fingers, unable to tear her gaze away. Irving had never done much with his hands, at least not when she was around. Usually he kept them folded on top of his ample belly, unless he was using them to guide his fork to his mouth.

Ethan looked up, one eyebrow cocking. "Well? Do you know how to dismount?"

Jeanne stiffened. "Why, yes, Sheriff. I was only waiting for your permission. After all, I'm your prisoner."

Without bothering to see how he reacted to her words, she kicked her right foot free from the stirrup and swung her leg over the horse's back. She'd worn her fullest skirt today, for modesty's sake, but now the wind caught at it and tried to lift the hem upward. She grabbed for her skirts, trying to smooth them down, and somehow her legs and her arms got tangled up. Her foot slipped and she fell backward, but before she could do more than let out a shriek, strong arms grabbed her from behind. Her hat hit his shoulder, knocking it down over her eyes, but she already knew who it was.

"Mrs. McAllister," Ethan's voice said above her. "You are the most troublesome prisoner I've ever taken care of."

Jeanne tried to disentangle her hand so that she could push her hat out of her face. By the time she had accomplished that much, he had freed her foot from the stirrup and pulled her the rest of the way out of the saddle, setting her onto her own two feet. Without another word, he turned and walked toward the store, seeming to assume that she would follow him.

And she didn't really have much choice—not unless she wanted him to leave her stranded.

She caught up with him as he pushed through the door. He had the decency to hold it open for her, and Jeanne lifted her chin as she stepped inside.

"Well, would you look who's back in town!" the man behind the counter called out, grinning. "I was beginning to wonder if you were ever coming back!"

"So was I." Ethan moved closer, and Jeanne trailed behind him. She felt like a child, clinging close to the security of her father, but Ethan was her only connection to anything familiar. She didn't like him, but sticking to his side brought a strange sense of comfort.

The storekeeper's eyes fell on her, and his eyebrows rose. "Is she with you, Ethan?"

"Yeah," Ethan said none too enthusiastically.

The storekeeper started to say more, but then a door opened behind him and a blond-haired woman stepped into the room, a child in her arms. "Well, Ethan, you made it back. Vivian was sure she heard your voice, but I didn't believe her."

The child stretched her arms toward Ethan, jabbering away, and Ethan grinned. He crossed the space between them in two strides and grabbed her out of the woman's arms, tossing the little girl up toward the ceiling. Jeanne gasped and clapped her hand over her mouth to smother the sound. Really, he ought to be more careful with the child.

But the little girl seemed to enjoy Ethan's antics, and she squealed. He settled her in his arms, and she grabbed a hold of his face with both hands, chattering with words Jeanne couldn't begin to understand. Ethan baby-talked right back to her, and Jeanne could only shake her head. What had happened to the stiff, unsmiling man she had met in Columbus?

Finally Ethan seemed to remember her and turned to face her again—and he was back to frowning. "This is my daughter, Vivian. And Vivian, this is Mrs. McAllister." He glanced toward the shopkeeper and the blond. "Oh, and that's Ephraim and Sadie Mayfield. They run this mercantile."

Sadie stepped forward, beaming. "I'm *so* happy to meet you, Mrs. McAllister. Are you planning to stay here long?"

Ethan answered for her. "Well, actually I was hoping you could help me on that. Mrs. McAllister lives in Columbus, but she's here to help me for a couple weeks. Since staying at my place definitely wouldn't be proper, I wondered if you might have room for her here. She has a horse she could ride out to the farm during the day—"

"Of course, she can stay here. I'll do anything I can to help out." Sadie smiled from Ethan to Jeanne.

"Sadie," Ethan said with almost a growl. "Don't look at us like that."

Sadie's eyes widened. "Like how?"

"Like you think we make a cute couple. I don't want to hear a word about it—understand?"

Jeanne gasped again. *A cute couple?* Her stomach began to churn at the very idea. Who in their right minds would think that she and Ethan made a nice pair?

Evidently Sadie. She grinned unrepentantly. "Oh, Ethan, don't be so touchy. How can you blame me for jumping to conclusions when you make such a nice match?"

An all-too-familiar feeling of nausea washed over Jeanne, and she knew it wasn't going to pass. Ethan was saying something, but she interrupted him and asked, "Where's the outhouse?"

Sadie must have sensed her urgency. "Right this way."

Jeanne followed her through the door behind the counter, focusing on breathing evenly and *not* on the look that Ethan must be wearing. Sadie moved quickly through what seemed to be her living apartment and outside to a wooden outhouse. Still, Jeanne had to run the final steps and throw the door open so that she was over the hole when her stomach heaved up its contents.

And here she had been doing so well today. She had even let herself think that she must be past the worst of the morning sickness, but now a tiny little trigger like being paired up with *Ethan Becker* had her in misery again.

When her stomach was under control again, Jeanne stepped out of the outhouse and found herself facing Sadie again.

"Are you all right?" Sadie asked, her forehead furrowed.

"Not really, but it will pass." Jeanne sighed and placed her hand over her middle. "I'm expecting."

"Ah, I see. Ethan called you 'Mrs.,' but I thought he made a slip of the tongue."

Jeanne shook her head. "No, Irving and I were married for less than a year, but definitely married."

"And how far into your pregnancy are you?"

"Ten weeks, as close as I can figure."

Sadie nodded. "That can be a rough spot to be in. But don't worry. I'm sure you'll start feeling better in no time. And as long as you're here in Osceola, you're welcome to stay with me and Ephraim."

"Thank you." Jeanne smiled at her, then grabbed her hat before a puff of hot wind could snatch it from her head. Terrible wind. She would have to find a better way to keep her hat where it belonged.

"Come inside and I'll get you a drink and maybe something to eat that will settle your stomach." Sadie motioned her to follow, then paused. "How long ago did your husband pass away?"

"Three weeks," Jeanne replied.

Sadie's expression fell. "Oh. Then I guess you won't be looking to remarry for a while."

"No," Jeanne almost whispered. No, she *never* wanted to find herself a married woman again.

4

"I'm sorry, sir, but you must be confused."

Jeanne gave the livery man her nicest smile, but he didn't melt a bit. Just stood there like a pillar of granite blocking the doorway to the barn, jaw working a chew of tobacco.

Jeanne tried again. "Really, I don't think you possibly could have understood Mr. Becker. How does he expect me to get to his farm without a horse?"

The livery man stared back at her and deliberately shifted his chew to the other side of his mouth. "Maybe you should have asked him."

Jeanne balled her fists at her side and released her breath in a huff. "But I'm supposed to be helping him. How does he expect me to do that if I'm stuck in town? It makes no sense."

"I think it makes perfect sense," a voice said behind her, and Jeanne spun around to find Ethan Becker himself, seated on his horse with Vivian in front of him. The little smile on his face made her wonder just how long he had been sitting there.

Recovering her composure, Jeanne pointed a finger at him.

"Do you really think it's safe to have a baby on a horse with you?"

Ethan's smile disappeared. "She's my child. And you have no say in what I do or don't do with her."

He dismounted and lifted Vivian down after him. He looked beyond Jeanne, and she saw that Mr. Liveryman had opened his barn and was bringing out her horse, fully saddled. She started to reach for the reins, but Mr. Liveryman walked right past her and placed the reins in Ethan's hands.

"What—?" Jeanne began, but Ethan sent her a look.

"Mrs. McAllister, let's get one thing straight between us. You are my responsibility, and as such, I cannot allow you to get into situations that may give you a chance to make a run for it. I don't suppose you could get too far on foot even if you tried, but a horse is another matter. I would catch you, but I'd rather avoid the trouble that would be involved in that for both of us. So from now on, if you want to be on horseback, you'll need to let me know in advance. You aren't setting a foot in the saddle unless I'm there to watch you."

He seemed to feel the matter was closed and set to work tying her horse to his.

Jeanne stared at him, a hot feeling gathering inside her. He thought *she* would try to break her word? Just how much lower could his opinion of her get?

"So how am I supposed to get to your place after today?" she asked, barely able to restrain her fury.

"Vivian and I will escort you." He looked back at her and had the nerve to smile. "Of course, there's no need for you to come here to the livery if you'd rather not. We're more than capable of fetching your horse for you."

She tried to speak, choked on her words, and then spun away and stormed over to her horse. As upset as she was, she had herself into the saddle in one bound.

Ethan tossed Vivian into the saddle again and scrambled up after her. He started their horses out of town, and Jeanne mentally made note of the day. *Thursday.* Just fourteen more days to endure—and she wasn't staying a day longer than she had to.

Escorting Jeanne McAllister to and from his place every day was going to add work to his life, but depending on how well she took care of Vivian and the house, Ethan had to admit that he didn't have the worst end of the bargain. She had snap and fire to her, but she seemed the decent sort. As long as she didn't try to run away, he wasn't worried about letting her into his house and placing his daughter in her care. At least, not too much.

He cast a glance back at her. He wouldn't put it past her to dig into him if given half a chance, but she seemed concerned about Vivian's well-being. A bit too smothering, but that could be dealt with.

"How long have you lived in Nebraska?" he asked. He wasn't trying to get to know her better; he just figured they might as well put the time to good use. That was all.

She sat a little stiffer. "Two years."

"Just two?"

"Yes, just two." She eyed him. "Why do you ask?"

"Thought you might want to talk."

Her lips tightened. "Not really. Not with you."

Ouch. There he went getting her all riled up again. He figured he had better quit before she got too mad.

He kept silent until they reached his farm, and then he glanced back at her, trying to gauge her expression. His homestead wasn't a bad little place in his estimation. He had poured a lot of work into improving it, especially the house, before Mamie died. Small trees that he had planted and watered were taking root in the yard. The fences were straight. The house painted. The porch even had two rockers.

Her face didn't change, and Ethan pulled his gaze away, an odd feeling of hurt welling inside his chest. Of course he had known she wouldn't like it. She didn't like anything about him. But for some reason, he had hoped she would say something positive about his place, at least acknowledge the work he had put into it.

He shrugged. Oh, well—it didn't matter. She was likely too highfalutin' to appreciate the simpler side of life.

They dismounted in front of the house, and Ethan led the way up the steps and through the door. The house didn't look too bad today, at least not in his opinion. He had tackled the mess in the kitchen the night before and gotten it mostly under control. Vivian's dress was clean, her diaper dry, and he felt pleased with himself. Now she would see just how fine he was getting along without a woman in his life, and maybe she would see fit to pass the message along to Sheriff Calaman and Judge Pratt when she returned to Columbus.

He looked her way and caught her biting her lip as she looked around. Now why would that be?

He followed her gaze around the kitchen. The floor *did* have quite a few boot prints tracked around the room, especially here in the doorway. The table *did* have some crumbs scattered across it—he had forgotten to wipe them off this morning. A couple pots he had forgotten to wash sat on the floor next to the stove—a pile of rags he had used to wipe up Vivian's milk spill sat on the chair—oh, and there was that dirty pair of pants he had dropped in the corner. He had planted his knee in a cow pie and forgotten to wash them up. Flies were buzzing around them now.

Mess seemed to sprout up before his eyes, and now *he* began to chew on his lower lip. He thought he got along well enough, but placing this impeccably dressed woman in the room made him realize just how far his standards had slipped since Mamie's death. She must think him a disaster.

"Guess I'll see you tonight," he mumbled, and setting Vivian on the floor, he made a fast retreat. Even Vivian's dress had a rip in its skirt—and he hadn't noticed. He would do well to get out of the house while he was still in one piece.

Jeanne refused to let herself smile until the door latched shut behind Ethan. Looking at the little girl on the floor, Jeanne clicked her tongue. "Vivian, honey, I don't know how either you or your papa can stand living in this house. It's a disgrace."

No wonder Judge Pratt was so convinced Ethan needed a wife.

She looked out the window and watched as Ethan rode away—still leading her horse. Well, he needn't worry about her trying to run away. What was there to run to? She'd been fired from the Columbus Hotel—and she couldn't make herself feel sorry about it. She had hated the job.

No, she really could be in a worse fix than this. Cleaning had never bothered her, and after sneaking a glance into the pantry, she smiled. Ethan had plenty of supplies on hand, and if she did come across an ingredient she needed—well, she would let him taste her cinnamon rolls, and then she figured he wouldn't fuss over a trip to the store. Irving hadn't.

"Vivian, we'll make this place shine, and we'll sweeten your papa up with a few desserts, and then maybe he'll stop calling me a criminal." Jeanne tapped Vivian's nose. "You do know that your papa is wrong about that, don't you?"

Vivian looked up at her through tangled hair and frowned. "No, no."

Her look imitated Ethan so well that Jeanne laughed in spite of herself.

"Oh, Vivian, your papa might know many things, but this is one time he's made a mistake. But don't worry. I'll have both of you convinced in no time."

Vivian's frown deepened, and Jeanne decided to leave her alone for now. She had plenty to do without getting the little girl worked into a tantrum.

Humming to herself, Jeanne took a peek into each room of the house, her confidence growing with each look. For all the fuss he had put up about not needing a woman, his house proved otherwise. She could hardly restrain her delight—but strangely enough, none of that delight was at Ethan's expense. No, actually she felt rather sorry for the man. She could see that he had tried to keep the place neat, but his efforts had failed. Even Vivian looked none too clean.

When it came right down to it, the real cause for her delight was because for the first time since cracking heads with Ethan in Columbus, she felt as if not quite every circumstance of her life was out of control. Placed here in her element in this dirty house, she would prove to Ethan that she had more character to her than he realized.

5

Jeanne couldn't help but wonder if Ethan had thought matters completely through before he arrived at the Mayfields' door, ready to escort her to church.

She knew he was thinking merely business. The no-nonsense look on his face announced more plainly than words that he intended to make sure she was seated in the church pew where she belonged and not making a desperate effort to escape—but she found it impossible to get over his words that he was "going to accompany her to church."

She tried to argue that she would attend with the Mayfields, but he wouldn't hear of it. As long as he was nearby, he seemed duty-bound to watch over her.

So she stopped arguing and let him guide her toward the church. Maybe things were different here, and maybe people wouldn't make the conclusions she imagined they would. And if they did—well, that was Ethan's problem.

The two-block walk from Mayfield Mercantile to the church passed almost too fast. Jeanne used her handkerchief to dab at a trickle of sweat as they neared the building, then tucked it back into her sleeve and pasted on a smile. No one would guess her real reasoning for being here in Osceola—she was sure of that. Her mauve dress swished around her dainty black shoes. Her hat sat at the perfect angle. She looked nice—she had checked the mirror to make sure she did.

She glanced at Ethan. He hadn't even noticed.

But there was no time to indulge in a pity party. Everyone in the churchyard was staring at them—and judging by the way the matrons' eyebrows were lifting, they didn't see her as the law-breaker Ethan did.

Jeanne felt the heat flood her face. The matrons were already descending, beaming smiles in place.

"Why, Ethan—who is this?" one elderly woman asked, cane tapping to keep up with her feet as she rushed forward.

Ethan frowned. "Jeanne McAllister."

"Ah, well—welcome to Osceola, dear."

The other women chimed in with their own greetings, and as they pressed closer, Ethan gripped Jeanne's arm as if he thought they might tear her away from him.

Jeanne smothered her groan as the women's faces softened and they exchanged looks that asked each other if they had noticed.

Ethan seemed to realize his mistake, and he released her as quickly as if he had grabbed onto fire. And just that fast, the women were shooing him away toward the men and pressing around Jeanne, their eyes almost starved as they fixed on her face.

"Oh, my dear, how did you ever catch hold of him?" one woman whispered, edging her way closest.

"Um—ah—" Jeanne looked toward Ethan, who had a most befuddled look on his face, and inwardly she seethed. She had known this would happen!

"I didn't think any woman was *ever* going to catch his attention," another woman spoke up.

"Well, Jeanne must have had a time of it," another one broke in. "Ethan had the art of ignoring young women down to perfection."

"But he only needed one to break through the barrier!"

"Oh, my dear, I'm so pleased I could burst. That child of his desperately needed a mama." The cane-bearing old woman beamed at her.

Jeanne stared from one woman to another, hardly able to think with all their chatter.

Then one woman sobered. "We've all been praying for this for a long time. You are our answer to prayer."

All the other women quieted as well, murmuring their agreement, and Jeanne's throat began to close. If they thought Ethan was smitten with her, they were in for a nasty shock. He had seemed surprised by all the cleaning she had accomplished over the past couple days, and he had seemed to enjoy the meals she had prepared for him and Vivian, along with her extra baking. But smitten? Not a chance. *Tolerating* was a better choice of words.

"It's about time he moved beyond Mamie and got on with his future," another woman said, and the other women nodded wisely.

Jeanne must have frowned, because the old lady with the cane patted her arm. "I suppose Ethan doesn't say much about Mamie, but those two were the most perfectly matched couple you ever did see. They adored one another, and it's no wonder he's had such a hard time getting over her death. You never saw such a beautiful woman as Mamie Becker. Lovely figure. Big blue eyes. Golden hair that curled just perfectly. She looked like an angel."

Jeanne's cheeks heated still more, and she almost reached up to touch her own straight brown hair. She caught herself just in time. No one had ever called *her* a beauty. Her hair was nothing special. Her eyes were a normal brown. And her waist was growing thicker by the day. Certainly not angelic.

The pastor appeared in the church doorway and tugged on the bell rope. The women's faces fell, and Jeanne exhaled the breath she had been holding. What a relief!

Ethan materialized almost out of nowhere, Vivian in his arms, and pointed toward the church. Jeanne dipped her head in a nod and trudged after him. She couldn't keep her eyes from straying to his broad shoulders—and she couldn't help but wonder about his Mamie.

So—he had been one of those lucky people with a love match. If he had really had that kind of a marriage, the kind that came only "once in a lifetime," as they said, then she thought everyone ought to stop plaguing him about getting married again. If he didn't have the heart to try again, then why should they force him to? It would have been kinder if they had stopped matchmaking and instead given him a little help, maybe by mending his laundry. Judging by the state his and Vivian's clothes had been in when she arrived, she knew they hadn't done that.

And she certainly didn't know why they had jumped to the conclusion that she and Ethan were—well—a couple. *She* didn't compare to his Mamie. She was the bane of his existence, and she knew he would be relieved when he could finally get her off his hands.

Jeanne sat down in the pew next to Ethan and Vivian, keeping her back straight and her chin high, Well, she could hardly wait to get away from here either. She didn't like being coupled with the town's fine-looking sheriff, and she didn't enjoy sitting here in this overly warm church trying to pretend that she didn't notice that everyone's eyes were fixed on her.

Only she wasn't sure of where she was going after this.

She glanced sideways at Ethan and Vivian. They offered her a measure of security for now, but what would happen when her two weeks were up? The days were already ticking off her countdown. *Eleven more days—*

After the service Ethan tried to get Vivian and Jeanne down the aisle and away from the church before the women could pounce on them again, but he should have known better than to try. Sadie caught hold of Jeanne and refused to let her get away without being introduced around, and as they disappeared into the crowd, Florence Hoffman found Ethan.

"Well, Ethan. Would you like to confirm if what the gossips are saying is true, or if there's another side to this story?"

Ethan heaved a sigh. "I guess you of all people should know that the gossips rarely have their facts right when it comes to me."

"It's easier to make assumptions than to take the time to find out the real facts," Florence said wisely.

"And facts are rarely as pleasant as those sweet assumptions." Ethan stared off toward the women clustered around Jeanne and frowned. He was glad he didn't know what nonsense about him they were filling her head with.

Florence patted his arm. "Well, here's your chance to tell one person how things really are."

Ethan sighed again and pulled his gaze back to his neighbor. "I haven't told anyone this, for Mrs. McAllister's sake if nothing else, but I know you won't gossip. You see, Mrs. McAllister is in trouble with the law."

Florence's eyes widened. "The law? Oh, Ethan—you're joking. She looks too innocent to be on the wrong side of the law. What did she do?"

Ethan thought back to the day he had met Jeanne at the Columbus Hotel, and he felt irritated all over again. "She threw roast dinner at Sheriff Calaman and me."

Florence's hand flew to her mouth and she burst into peals of laughter.

Ethan stared at her. "It wasn't funny. And to make matters worse, she couldn't pay her fine, so Judge Pratt decided to use her as a pawn to make me realize that my life would be better off with a woman in it. So now I've got eleven more days to deal with her before she goes back to Columbus."

Florence shook her head at him, her mouth still quirked upward. "Ah, Ethan, you really are a stubborn case, aren't you? Even Judge Pratt's opinion can't sway you."

"No, I might be stubborn, but I'm not stupid. I don't want another woman in my life, and the faster Mrs. McAllister gets on her way, the sooner life can return to normal."

Florence shook her head again, but her smile had vanished. "I know you don't want to hear this, but I think you *would* be better off if you remarried. You and Vivian both would do better with a woman in your home. What kind of a childhood will Vivian have when she's bounced from one neighbor's home to another while you're at work? God has a created order for families, and taking the woman out of the equation doesn't work so well."

"Well, death isn't supposed to happen either, but it did, and now I can't change that." Ethan's gaze wandered back toward Jeanne. "I just don't know how those women could think I'd be smitten with her. She's all pepper and spice."

"But very lovely."

Ethan shrugged. "Hadn't noticed."

"Why, Ethan Becker! Lying?" Florence narrowed her eyes. "Come now—'fess up like a good boy and admit the truth."

"Well, she's not beautiful in the same way that Mamie was." His own words put an uncomfortable feeling in his middle. Now why had he gone and compared Jeanne to Mamie? When it came right down to it, Mamie's beauty had been too fake for his liking. Too forced. And Florence knew how he felt.

"I don't think I even need to reply to that." Florence's smile told him that she knew he was aware of the spot he had put himself in. "There are different kinds of beauty, and this girl has the type that comes from within, the kind that reveals a beautiful character." She leaned closer. "Of course, her hair is quite attractive as well. All those pretty highlights in it—"

Ethan clamped his mouth shut and folded his arms across his chest. She wasn't going to bait him into agreeing with her.

Florence laughed. "You can't fool me, Ethan. You have eyes, and I know that you see what I'm talking about." She lowered her voice. "And do you want to know something else?"

"What?" Ethan asked in spite of himself.

"I don't know the circumstances, but I'm glad that girl threw roast dinner at you."

"What!" Ethan straightened, but Florence held out a hand.

"Maybe Judge Pratt is right, and now that you've had a woman forced back into your house, you'll realize how much you need one. And maybe, just *maybe,* this girl will be the answer herself."

"But she's too—"

"I know. You said she was too peppery, but if she's going to put up with you for any length of time, she'll need some spunk. I've had my eye on you, Ethan, and don't think I haven't noticed the way you act whenever a young woman gets within throwing distance of you. You get all stiff and no-nonsense, and you intimidate her from even trying to say hello to you." Florence shook her head. "You have a completely twisted view of women, and until you get that straightened out, I'll encourage that little lady at your house to do whatever she needs to, even if it means throwing more roast dinners at you."

And before he could say a word, Florence turned and walked away.

Ethan frowned after her. He had thought she was better than most women in Osceola about sticking her nose into his business, but here she had gone and proved him wrong. She was the *worst* of them all.

And it didn't help that her words pricked him like none of the other women's did.

6

The house must have missed two full years of spring and fall cleanings. The layer of dust confirmed it.

Jeanne stepped back to admire the now-empty cupboards that she had finished scrubbing. She had rewashed the dishes as well, and everything except her rag and wash water looked squeaky clean. Besides that, she had Ethan and Vivian's supper in the oven: ham and cornbread and berry cobbler. That dessert had been her main priority today. Ethan needed something to sweeten him up given the way he had been acting since church yesterday.

Jeanne sighed. She had tried to warn him and he hadn't listened, so he needn't act snappish with her. But it did no good to tell him that.

Returning to work, Jeanne organized the dishes—only more to her taste, not the way they had been organized before. Honestly, who'd had the idea of putting the frying pans in the farthest cupboard from the stove? That just made no sense. And the plates would be handier if they were stacked closer to the dish basin, and the cups would be better on a lower shelf—

Humming, Jeanne set each dish in the cupboard just so. She felt like a little girl playing house, only this was even more fun. With Ethan gone, she could imagine this was her own house and this was her own kitchen. She could even make Vivian her own daughter, and sometimes as she worked, she chatted with Vivian about the baby on the way and how they would have so much fun together—even if the truth was that she would be long gone by the time her baby entered the world. Still, Vivian liked the game, and sometimes Jeanne let her put her hand on her stomach to "feel the baby," even though it would be a while before the baby was big enough that either of them could feel any movement.

The playacting made life seem the next thing to perfect—until Ethan arrived home and shattered it. Somehow just the sight of his face brought reality crashing back on her with all its harsh facts, and she knew that her dream world would stay just out of her grasp until tomorrow when he left her and Vivian alone again.

But why spoil the present with gloomy thoughts? Jeanne shook her head to dislodge her worries, but the movement only dislodged her foot from the step stool. With a shriek, Jeanne dropped the mugs in her hand and grabbed the cupboard door with both hands. She landed on her right foot, twisting sideways, and the cupboard door let out a squeal.

Oh no. Forcing her chin up, Jeanne looked at the cupboard. Her heart sank. The whole door hung at an odd angle, and the top hinge had pulled free from the wood. Added to that, the remains of four mugs littered the countertop.

Jeanne blew out a breath and looked up at the ceiling. "Oh, boy—how will I explain this to Ethan?"

Well, maybe if she could fix it herself, she wouldn't have to tell him. At least about the cupboard door. She could do nothing about the mugs, so she would have to confess that much to him.

Now where did Ethan keep his tools? She turned, and who should be standing in the doorway but Ethan himself?

Jeanne's heart nearly stopped. She was in trouble now.

Ethan's eyes took in the mess of the kitchen and settled on the dangling cupboard door. He said nothing, and Jeanne's middle tightened. Papa had always gotten really quiet like that when he was furious.

At last Ethan spoke. "Mrs. McAllister, you may not like being here, but there's no need to tear my house apart."

His words took a moment to register in Jeanne's mind. Wait, was he saying—?

"Mr. Becker." Jeanne drew herself up to her full height. "I can assure you that I did *not* intend to break your cupboard door. It was an accident."

His expression didn't change. "I see—just like pitching a plate of roast dinner onto my shirtfront was an accident."

"Yes, exactly like that." Jeanne made herself look him squarely in the eye and refused to flinch. Stubborn man! Would he ever see the light? The way he acted, she may as well have taken a knife to him that day in the Columbus Hotel.

Ethan shook his head, blowing out a breath much as she had done when she saw the damage she had caused the cupboard door. "Mrs. McAllister, please—could you just control yourself for ten more days?"

So he was keeping a countdown too. He probably was counting the hours until he could get her off his hands. Trying to ignore the sting the thought gave her, Jeanne lifted her chin. "Mr. Becker, I am *not* out of control of myself, nor am I out to get you, and by the time we're freed from one another, I believe you will be obliged to admit that."

Whirling back to the bare cupboards, Jeanne picked up a stack of pots and shoved them into place more loudly than necessary. Ethan Becker *would* see the light if she had to pry his eyes open herself.

But when she risked a glance back at him, he was still watching her with narrowed eyes. Her words seemed to have done nothing to convince him that she didn't have it in for him.

Nine more days on the countdown—

Jeanne arranged the last gingersnap cookie on the plate and smiled. "Gingersnaps are my favorite kind of cookie, Vivian. My papa's too. He could eat a whole pan of them all by himself."

"Papa?" Vivian looked up at Jeanne with blue eyes, small hands gripping the back of the chair she had pulled up to the counter to stand on.

"Ah, I said the magic word, didn't I?" Jeanne picked up the plate, then adjusted a cookie just a little farther to the left. Perfect. "Well, I hope your papa likes gingersnaps too. Maybe it will help him get over what I did to the cupboard door."

"Your tactics are a little too obvious," a voice said from behind her shoulder, and with a scream, Jeanne whirled around. Cookies flew from the plate in her hand, forming a perfect arc as they sailed through the air and pelted into Ethan.

"Oh, I—you—how did you get through the door so quietly?" Jeanne stammered, pressing her hand to her racing heart.

Ethan looked down at the cookie crumbles at his feet, then deliberately lifted his eyes to hers. He looked miffed, almost as if he thought she had hit him with the cookies on purpose.

That was yet another mark against her.

Just eight more days—

Jeanne swiped the back of her hand across her forehead to get the sweat out of her eyes, then sat back on her heels to look at the floor. She couldn't deny that she felt pleased with herself. She had used her grandma's recipe for cleaning floors, and the kitchen and dining room *did* look lovely. All the ugly scratches and boot scuffs had disappeared, and the wood looked as if new life had been breathed into it. It would look even nicer once she took a rag to remove most of the wax.

She smiled. Floor-waxing day used to be her favorite time to visit her Grandma Larson, because Grandma always let her slide around on the wood just before she took her rag to it. The wax made the floor almost as good for sliding as ice.

Picking up her rag, Jeanne set to work buffing out the wax but paused when she heard the door open. Ethan was home already? She looked out the window and bit her lip. Time must have gotten away from her. The sun hung low enough that he *must* be back.

"Take your boots off before you come in here!" she called, working her rag faster across the floor.

Silence rang from the doorway, but at last she heard the thump of first one boot, and then the other hitting the porch floor.

"Mrs. McAllister?" The kitchen floorboards creaked as he stepped inside.

"In the dining room. Be careful. I just finished waxing the—"

A crash came from the kitchen, followed by a muffled groan. "Mrs. McAllister!"

Jeanne put her hand to her head and muttered, "I tried to warn you, Mr. Becker. I tried."

That was her second mark in two days.

Seven more days left on the countdown—only one more week—

Jeanne planted a fist in her aching back, her heart feeling sicker than it had any day so far. Her time was halfway up, and she was still no closer to figuring out what she would do after her time with Ethan was up. Seven days had gone by fast—and the next week was bound to go even faster.

Please, Lord—show me what Your next plan for me is. I'm clean out of options.

Jeanne looked up at the sky, then felt silly. She had no doubt that God had heard her prayer, but she rather doubted He would drop a sign from heaven or arrange the clouds into a special message for her. No, she would just have to give Him time to see what He would do. Sometimes His answers came at the last moment with no prior warning—not exactly a comforting thought. But His answers were never too late and would come at just the right time.

Hefting up her bucket of dirty scrub water—the pantry had undergone her cleaning attack today—Jeanne decided to take the lazy option and walked to the edge of the porch to dump it. If she had felt more ambitious, she would have doled it out among the plants in the garden, but she was tired enough that she couldn't summon the will to care that she was being wasteful.

Jeanne got a grip on the handle and the bottom of the bucket, then pitched the water over the railing. At the last moment, something caught the periphery of her vision, but it was too late. The water was out of the bucket and arcing through the air—right on top of Ethan.

He caught the full brunt of her deluge, and grimy water washed over his hat, his face, his shirt, and all the way down to his boots. The shock of it seemed to render him mute, and with her hand against her throat, Jeanne watched his face as he coughed on water, blinked it out of his eyes, then coughed some more. Then he just stood there, his eyes drilling into her and rooting her to the spot.

She endured the silence for as long as she could but finally couldn't stand it. "Um, Mr. Becker, I didn't know you were home." She forced out a laugh, but it sounded off to her own ears.

He inhaled, and she braced herself for his tongue lashing, but then he exhaled.

"That excuse is a little old, Mrs. McAllister," he said, his voice controlled but frigid.

"Mr. Becker, you can't honestly think I meant to hit you with that water." She forced out another laugh, but when the look on his face didn't change, she tried again. "I *am* sorry, Mr. Becker, but you can't blame me. I don't know why you were sneaking around the side of the house, but I didn't see you."

"I wasn't sneaking," he said, all but growling. "I heard one of the chickens putting up a fuss behind the house, so I went to check on it. My horse is tied up front, so don't pretend like you didn't know I was home."

"But I didn't see your horse. Call me what you like, but sometimes I get too focused on my task and don't pay attention to my surroundings. It was an accident."

"Hmm." Ethan shifted his position and folded his arms. "All your—*accidents*—are so well timed that it's uncanny, Mrs. McAllister. Real uncanny."

Well, of all the nerve! Jeanne started to speak, then looked at him again and thought better of it. He really was in a sorry state, standing there with his wet clothes clinging to him and water still dripping from his hat. The grime had left streaks down his face, and Jeanne couldn't feel angry with him. She *had* just dumped a bucket of scrub water on him. Irving would have been hopping with rage if he had been the one in Ethan's fix.

Still, Ethan might not be yelling or throwing things, but something smoldered in his eyes that told Jeanne he wasn't going to be forgetting—or forgiving—anytime soon.

She had made another mark against herself—and she was so sick of her own accidents that she felt like railing right along with Ethan.

7

Keeping a wary eye out for the feisty little Mrs. McAllister, Ethan left his horse tied in front of the house and climbed the porch steps. No flying buckets of water yet. So far so good.

He cracked the door open and called, "Mrs. McAllister!" No way was he getting any closer to her in the kitchen than he had to. Bad things always happened when they got too close to one another around food.

No answer came from the house, and after hollering her name again, he turned and studied the farm, frowning. She couldn't have gone too far. Not with Vivian in tow.

But searching the farm from the front porch didn't uncover his blond-haired daughter or the brown-and-sorta-reddish, sorta-goldish-haired woman who had a knack for getting under his skin like no other woman. *Only six more days now.*

Why didn't that bring him the relief he had thought it would?

Sighing, he walked down the steps and took off toward the barn. Of course, when the little lady wasn't beating up on him, she seemed like the handy kind of person to have around. He hadn't missed the way she had gotten his house under control again, or the extra goodies she made for him and Vivian. Vivian seemed to think Jeanne made the sun rise and set, and she jabbered a mile a minute about her, asking when she would be back and saying some nonsense about a baby. He wasn't sure what those two had been up to—maybe playing tea party with Vivian's baby doll.

The thought pricked at him. He had done well at spending time with his daughter—taking her on errands with him, riding the horse, taking walks through the pasture. But he had never thought about a tea party or any of those other "girl" things she ought to be enjoying if Mamie were alive. Just the week before, he had come home to find Vivian and Jeanne pulling cookies out of the oven—cookies with faces that Vivian had created out of dried berries. He had watched from the doorway, listening to their laughter and noticing how good Jeanne was with Vivian. No wonder Vivian was so taken with her. Jeanne was providing her with the things only a woman would think to give.

He did appreciate all that Jeanne did—he just couldn't think of how he could say it without condoning all her well-timed "accidents." He snorted. How could she think he would be so naïve as to believe she hadn't meant to get at him with all those attacks?

Laughter floated toward him from behind the chicken coop, and he switched direction to head that way. He rounded the corner and quickly spotted them. They were walking his way, Vivian on Jeanne's hip, both of them wearing flowers in their hair and matching smiles.

Vivian saw him first. "Papa!" she cried, wiggling for Jeanne to set her down.

Ethan grinned and held out his arms. He would never get tired of her enthusiasm at seeing him.

Jeanne followed more slowly, her smile wiped from her face. Really, she looked almost upset to see him.

Was she? Surely she didn't dislike him that much.

But then, why not? He had never made an effort to make himself likeable around her—in fact, maybe Florence *had* been right when she said that he liked intimidating young women into keeping their distance from him. Jeanne probably thought he was just a hard-cored man who delighted in dragging young women to court trials.

It bothered him, but he couldn't have said why. He wanted Jeanne to keep her distance. He didn't want her getting close to him—he didn't want to think about her more than he already was.

Jeanne looked up, her eyes catching his, and suddenly Ethan found his vision working even more sharply than normal. Her eyes really were a nice shade of brown, almost a hazel color. She dropped her gaze, lowering her lovely dark lashes. A bit of a smile touched her lips, and she looked up at him again, a sparkle in her eyes. It did wonders to her face. Ethan couldn't tear his gaze away, and he almost couldn't focus as her lips formed a single word. "Chicks."

Slowly the word worked its way into his mind, and Ethan blinked, wondering if he had heard her right. "What?"

"Chicks," she said again, pointing to Vivian. "That's what she's trying to tell you."

Vivian had been talking to him? He hadn't even noticed.

He felt heat creeping up his collar, and he quickly focused his attention on Vivian, hoping Jeanne wouldn't notice.

Vivian jabbered away at him again, and sure enough, he caught the words *chick* and *baby*.

"Oh, really?" he said, trying *not* to think of Florence's words about beauty, both inward and outward, and above all, her comment about Jeanne having both kinds.

Vivian wiggled to get out of his arms, and he set her down. She latched onto his hand and started tugging him forward.

"Where are we going?" he asked, fully aware that she was leading him straight toward Jeanne.

Jeanne grinned, and he thought for sure she had read his thoughts—until she said, "Come on, Vivian. Let's show your papa what we found."

She grabbed Vivian's other hand, and Ethan found himself staring at the wedding ring on her finger. Her husband was dead—but she still wore it. He gave his head a slight shake. Time he got his head on straight again. Just because Jeanne and Vivian fit together so well was no reason to go getting any crazy ideas. Sheriff Calaman had told him that Jeanne's husband had been gone only a few weeks, and besides that, he didn't want another woman in his life. A woman was a tiny little thing, but when she took over a man's life, she sure brought plenty of bags of trouble with her. He knew that much, and he wouldn't be forgetting it anytime soon.

"See, Papa, see!" Vivian was saying, tugging on his arm again, and Ethan crouched down beside her. There, almost blending in with the grass, he saw a brown hen, and he smiled when he heard a faint cheeping sound. A yellow head peeped out from under the hen's wing, and Ethan hugged Vivian against him.

"Well, would you look at that! We've got baby chicks, don't we?"

"Baby chickies," Vivian repeated, beaming.

"I can't believe how cute they are," Jeanne said, and looking sideways at her, Ethan saw that she had crouched down too and wore a smile that about beat Vivian's.

"Ever seen chicks?" he asked, and she shook her head, making the flowers in her hair bob.

"No. I spent most of my life in the city." She met his gaze almost shyly. "This is the closest to a farm I've ever been."

She had mentioned that before, but he wasn't expecting the disappointment that cut through him this time. He tried to cover it with a smile. "Bet it's pretty different than what you're used to."

She shrugged. "In some ways, yes. In others, no. Houses clean about the same whether you're in the city or the country. But it's definitely more peaceful here." She looked down again. "I guess I rather like that."

But for how long? He had to bite his tongue to keep the question from slipping out. Yeah, he had met girls who liked the country for a time—but it wore off fast. Take Mamie, for instance.

Almost without conscious thought, he eased back from her, putting a little more distance between them. Nothing wrong with a little distance—and it could save a lot of heartache in the end.

8

Three more days until she left. Just three.

Jeanne rested her head against the back of the rocker on the porch. Vivian slumped against her, fast asleep, and Jeanne tapped her foot to keep the rocker in motion. She had thought her life was spinning out of control when Judge Pratt ordered her to come here, but now she was sure that God had known what He was doing all along. As she had told Ethan on Friday, it was peaceful here. And given the chaos of her last year, she had been in more desperate a need for peace than she had realized.

But all good things had to end at some point.

Motion at the end of the lane caught the corner of her eye, and she lifted her head a bit to look. *Ethan.* He didn't even need to get close for her to know it was him. The way he sat his saddle—comfortably yet with straightness to his posture that reminded her that he was a lawman with responsibilities—told her that right away.

She eased back in her seat, letting her eyes follow him as he drew closer to the house. He cut a fine figure up on his horse. Of course, Ethan Becker cut a fine figure *wherever* he went. Especially when he smiled. She had seen enough of his frowns that she could appreciate his smile.

He reined in his horse and dismounted in front of the house. "What, sitting on the job, Mrs. McAllister?" he asked, sending her one of those smiles she had just been admiring.

She felt her face heat—and it wasn't because of his words. "Ah, yes—well, Vivian was fussy, so I sat down to rock her, and she fell asleep—"

"Don't apologize. I was joking." Ethan tied his horse, then walked closer and sat down on the top step, sighing. "Truth is, I don't mind sitting down for a spell either."

He took off his hat, and Jeanne noticed that the lines of his face were cut a bit deeper than usual. "Long day?" she asked, surprising herself. She never made the effort to create small talk with him.

He didn't act as if she had said anything out of the ordinary. "It was long enough. Everyone seemed to think they had to visit the sheriff's office on the same day and report all their troubles." He sighed again and rubbed his hand against his face. "Some days I wonder why I thought I'd like to be the sheriff."

"Why did you?" Jeanne had never thought to wonder before, but looking around the farm, she knew he would have plenty to keep him busy here even if he weren't the county sheriff.

Ethan dropped his hand to his knee and met her gaze. "My Grandpa Becker was a sheriff." He smiled. "Guess he was about the biggest hero in my life. He's been dead for a long time now, but—well, I feel closer to him when I'm wearing a badge. Sorta as if I'm carrying on his legacy."

"It's a noble job."

"I suppose." Ethan leaned back against the railing. "What about you? How long had you been working at the Columbus Hotel?

"Six days."

"Six days?" His eyebrows rose. "Guess you hadn't been at it for too long."

"No. Irving had only been dead for three weeks." She looked down. "It took me a few days after the funeral to get his accounts straightened out. And when I did, that pretty much made my decision for me." She shrugged. "Of course, it could have been worse."

"Worse?" Ethan's eyebrows lowered.

"He could have been in debt. It happens a lot over the gaming tables." Too late, she caught herself and clapped her free hand over her mouth, her cheeks burning. She wasn't proud to be known as a gambler's wife.

But when she risked a glance at Ethan, she saw no condemnation in his eyes—just understanding. "I suppose it does," he said quietly. "I'm glad you didn't have to pay for his mistakes."

She felt as if a burden had slid off her shoulders. "It wasn't that Irving was a bad man. He always made sure there was plenty of food on the table, and—and—" She tried to think of any more redeeming qualities he had possessed. "And—um—he treated me pretty well most of the time."

"Most of the time?" Ethan's eyes narrowed still more, and Jeanne knew her effort to cast Irving in a better light had failed.

"Well, he did have a bit of a temper, he yelled a lot, and he smashed some things around, but he never hit *me,* if that's what you're wondering."

"Mm." Ethan eased back again, but he was still frowning. "So what possessed you to marry the man? Was he handsome?"

"Ah—maybe he was at one time," Jeanne hedged. "He was rather—out of his prime by the time I met him."

"Out of his prime?" Ethan's eyebrows rose. "What does that mean?"

"Well, he—he was bald. And a little round." Jeanne nibbled her lip. "But he couldn't help it—at least not the baldness. He was about my father's age."

"Your father's age?" Ethan sat up straighter. "Then why'd you marry him, for pity's sake?"

Jeanne blew out her breath. He wasn't going to let her evade the truth. "My father made me. He had this—idea, you see, that women's minds are too weak to handle money. He was dying, and he worried about what would become of me after he was gone. He had accumulated a small fortune over the years, and he feared some man would try to take advantage of me. So he married me to his good friend Irving McAllister."

Ethan said nothing, just stared at her with a look in his eyes that made her squirm. At last he said, "Well, that's one of the most low-down things I've ever heard of."

Jeanne pursed her lips. "They only did what they thought would be best for me. Papa wanted me to be happy, but his ideas were just—different, I guess."

Ethan shook his head. "It must have grated on you to have no choice in the matter."

"My papa was dying. I felt nothing except fear." Jeanne shrugged and looked away. "Besides, it wasn't so bad. There was no other man I wanted to marry, and I thought Irving and I might—well, at least look after one another."

"You mean *you* would look after *him* in his old age." Ethan shook his head again. "Of course he was happy to marry you. What old man wouldn't be pleased to come into possession of a beautiful young woman who was obliged to take care of him?"

Jeanne's heart stopped for one tiny second, then began to pound faster than if she had been racing. Had he just called her beautiful? Surely he didn't mean that.

Ethan must have mistaken her silence for something else. "I'm sorry," he said, his voice losing some of its edge. "I had no call to say that. I'm sure Irving found you more than just beautiful and convenient."

Jeanne shook her head. "No. He felt nothing more for me than just that—I was convenient." Her eyes fell to her lap. "And I didn't love him either."

Jeanne waited for him to speak, maybe to scold her for thinking such a thing, but he went quiet. She looked up at him again and found his dark eyes studying her, a little furrow in his forehead.

"I don't blame you if you think that sounds terrible," she said quickly. "I know you probably can't understand—"

"Can't understand?" Ethan's eyes didn't leave her face. "What makes you think I can't understand?"

"Well—" Jeanne began, then caught herself. From what everyone said, Ethan was still in deep mourning over his wife's passing. It would be heartless of her to bring his wife up now.

"I see. I couldn't understand your loveless marriage because I had the most perfect marriage this side of heaven—is that it?" Ethan asked.

Jeanne hesitated.

"Thought so." He leaned back against the railing, cocking one eyebrow at her. "I suppose the ladies at church told you all the ins and outs of my marriage to Mamie, didn't they?"

"Not *all* the ins and outs." Jeanne felt her face warm. Goodness, they hadn't been gossiping about him—well, not much anyway. "They only said that you and your wife were a perfect match and you adored each other and that you'd had a hard time getting over her death."

"I thought as much." Ethan sounded almost irritated. "I've heard all the comments about me and Mamie being passionately in love and deliriously happy. Funny thing is that none of those women ever asked me or Mamie if that's how we really felt. They made assumptions."

Jeanne watched him, trying to follow his train of thought. "So they're wrong?"

Ethan fidgeted with his hat. "I suppose it's partly my own fault, but yes, they're wrong."

"Oh." Jeanne wondered if she should apologize, but Ethan spoke again.

"I knew they could never understand, so I've let them think that Mamie and I were in love, but it's a lie." He sent her the briefest glance. "You were honest with me, so I guess it's only fair that I act the same toward you. I knew Mamie for my whole life—our families were good friends. In fact, our parents wanted to see us married so badly that you might say it was even arranged from our births. I knew their expectations, and I guess—well, I figured they ought to know best, so I never let myself think of anything besides marrying Mamie."

Jeanne nodded. She understood parents' expectations all too well.

Ethan drew in a deep breath. "Marrying Mamie was fixed so firmly in my mind that I didn't pay attention to all our differences. She was a town girl—I was just a farm boy. She was an only child used to always getting her own way—I was the youngest of nine, and I'd been taught to get along with the bare necessities. And then, of course, there were our dreams. We never discussed them before our wedding day, but I wanted to farm, while she wanted to move to an even bigger city and have her husband work for some fancy corporation. Of course, our parents hovered over our shoulders during our courtship, always steering the conversation away from any of those difficult—and important—conversations, so it's no wonder we found ourselves walking down the aisle together."

He shrugged. "I think we both had a bad feeling about it even during the wedding. Later Mamie told me that she had never even wanted me to come calling on her. She'd had her eye on another boy, but he left town after news got around that I was courting her."

Jeanne could only stare at him. She couldn't imagine any woman in her right mind being upset about marrying Ethan Becker. He was so—perfect.

"We moved out here, and she tolerated it at first but hated the farm more with every passing day—even though I built her the nicest house I could afford." He shrugged again. "I don't think either of us wanted to admit just how miserable we were, so we plastered smiles on our faces and pushed through."

He didn't speak again, and finally Jeanne asked, "How did she die?"

"She died giving birth to Vivian."

"Oh." Jeanne tightened her grip on Vivian, and almost in spite of herself, she placed her other hand over her own unborn baby. The thought of dying in childbirth had never occurred to her.

She didn't want to hear more, but Ethan was still talking, his eyes on a crack in the porch boards. "It happened fast. Mamie always bled easily. She'd get the smallest cut, and it would bleed and bleed." He paused. Almost to himself he said, "I had thought the baby might change things between us, help us grow closer. I thought she might as least forgive me for chasing away her first choice. Thought we would get more comfortable with one another. But . . ." His voice trailed off.

"I'm sorry," Jeanne said quietly.

He looked up from the crack he had been studying and gave her a tired smile. "It probably wouldn't have worked anyway."

Neither of them spoke for a long moment. Jeanne's rocker creaked, and Vivian stirred in her arms.

"We should probably get going," Jeanne said. The sun hung lower in the sky, and she knew it was past time that Sadie would be expecting her back.

Ethan stood, but his words weren't what she expected. "Ever thought of getting married again?"

"Me?" Jeanne stared back it him. "Irving hasn't even been dead for a month. I haven't had time to consider such a thing."

"Just wondered." Ethan shrugged almost self-consciously.

"Have *you*?" Jeanne asked. He had asked *her*, so she figured it was only fair.

Ethan shook his head. "I wouldn't want to even if there were a woman willing to take me."

Jeanne raised her eyebrows. "So you don't think Judge Pratt's prescription is good?"

"Not for me. I don't know why Pratt is so insistent that I find another wife, but I don't think I need one."

"I see." Jeanne shifted Vivian in her arms and stood up. "Well, I guess it's your choice."

"Mm hmm. Just wish everyone else would figure that out." Ethan glanced her way. "But I guess their matchmaking may have some benefits."

"Oh?"

"If Judge Pratt weren't so focused on making me see my need to remarry, he wouldn't have sent you here. And if he hadn't sent you here, my house would still be mess. Besides, those cinnamon rolls of yours are the best I've ever tasted."

Jeanne was sure her eyes must have gone wide. So he *had* noticed all that she had done—and he appreciated it. The knowledge put a feeling lighter than clouds in her middle, and she vowed that before she left, she would find the time to make another batch of cinnamon rolls.

Really, why had she ever thought that Ethan Becker was such a bad man?

9

"All right, Vivie—eat your snack and drink your milk quickly before your papa comes home." Jeanne set the cookie and milk on the table, then eased herself into the chair next to Vivian. She didn't know why she felt so tired. She hadn't done *that* much today.

At least her morning sickness was mostly gone. She had thought it would never pass, but her stomach had been acting up less often, to her relief.

Vivian started climbing into her chair, then changed her mind and ran from the kitchen.

"Vivian!" Jeanne called, planting her hand on the table. Now she would have to stand up again and go after her.

But before Jeanne could summon the willpower to get out of the chair, Vivian pattered back into the room, rag doll tucked under her arm. "Baby," she announced proudly.

Jeanne smiled. "Ah, you found your baby, didn't you?"

Vivian bobbed her head in a nod, then thrust her hand at Jeanne's stomach. "Baby?"

"Right—that's where my baby is." Jeanne put her hand over her stomach as well. "It will stay there for a little while longer, and then we'll be able to hold it."

Too late she remembered that Vivian would never get to hold her baby, but Vivian had already latched onto the word. "Hold? Hold?"

Jeanne swallowed. "When it's born—and if I see you again—you can hold my baby."

For a two-year-old, her words were satisfactory. Baby doll still under her arm, Vivian scrambled up into her seat and sat down to eat her snack. Jeanne couldn't keep up with her jabber, but she caught the word *baby* and smiled again. Too bad Ethan didn't intend to marry again. Vivian would love being a big sister.

Boots thudded on the steps, and Jeanne looked to Vivian. "Sounds like your papa is home."

Vivian's face lit up in a grin, and she wiggled down from her seat again to run to meet him. Jeanne felt an odd sense of eagerness herself, but she restrained herself from running to open the door for him. Acting too eager to see him again wasn't appropriate, for pity's sake!

The handle turned, and Jeanne vacated the table to straighten the few items out of place in the kitchen. Still, she was hard pressed not to turn to look as Ethan's voice said, "There's my girl!" and Vivian squealed.

Only tomorrow is left. Just tomorrow—and then I'll never see Ethan or Vivian again. Why did that thought tear at her heart almost as if she were losing family?

Jeanne shook her head, busying her hands with cleaning up the kitchen and trying to drown out her own thoughts. She barely heard Vivian jabbering away at Ethan, but then Ethan's voice broke through.

"Baby?" he was saying, his voice amused. "Yep, you sure do love that baby doll, don't you?"

"Baby," Vivian said again, wiggling to get down.

Ethan put her on the floor, and she pointed toward Jeanne. "Baby," she repeated.

Jeanne's heart about stopped pounding. Gracious, she was trying to tell Ethan about the baby on the way! She wasn't sure why, but she hadn't wanted Ethan to know. Sharing that information with him just seemed too—well, as if it would be one more tie linking them together. And ties were the last thing she needed with her upcoming departure tomorrow.

She couldn't look at Ethan. He was good at understanding Vivian's baby chatter—even better than her. There was no doubt he understood Vivian's meaning.

But Ethan's voice was just as relaxed as it had been before. "Was Mrs. McAllister playing with you and your baby? That was nice of her. You tell her thank you, all right?"

Vivian frowned a bit, but she dutifully turned to Jeanne. "Tank oo."

Jeanne began breathing again. So he hadn't guessed. It was just as well.

Ethan moved farther into the room and set a jar on the table. Whatever the grayish stuff in the jar was looked entirely unappetizing, and Jeanne frowned. "What's that?"

Ethan had already bent down to say something to Vivian about the doggie, so Jeanne moved closer, reading the label on the jar: *fermented herring.*

"What is that stuff?" she asked again, but now Ethan was walking into the kitchen to take a look in the oven. She could have sworn he was covering a smirk.

She let out a huff. So he didn't want to answer. She would have to find out on her own.

Grabbing the jar, she unscrewed the lid. Someone must have already opened it because it gave easily. But whatever *fermented herring* was certainly couldn't have been food, because the smell that emanated from the jar was putrid, almost like rotting fish carcasses—and its stench filled the whole room.

Jeanne clapped the lid back on, but she wasn't fast enough. A wave of nausea washed over her, and she knew there was no time to make it to the outhouse. She lunged for the ash bucket sitting next to the stove and promptly lost all the contents of her stomach. She stayed crouched where she was for a moment, panting, and then caught another whiff of the nasty smell and was back to heaving over the bucket again.

At last, with nothing left in her stomach to lose and some even breathing to get herself relaxed again, Jeanne risked a glance behind her. The jar had disappeared from the table, and the door stood wide open to let in more fresh air. Ethan was fidgeting with the window, trying to get it to open even farther.

He looked back at her, his forehead furrowed. "Are you all right?"

"I'm fine." Jeanne released her breath. "Just fine."

Ethan left the window and grabbed a chair from the table, pulling it over to her. "Here—sit down for a minute."

She didn't argue. He gripped her elbow to help her up, and she sat down in the chair with another sigh. She couldn't look at him. His opinion of her now must be incredibly low.

"I'm sorry," Ethan said, his words catching her by surprise.

Without raising her head, she lifted her eyes to look at him.

"I shouldn't have let you open that jar. I knew better. Forgive me?"

His eyes told her he meant his apology, and at the warmth that flooded through her at the thought of his caring about *her*, Jeanne lowered her eyes again. "Of course, I forgive you. I just don't know what you were doing with such disgusting stuff in the first place."

"Johan and Selma Olberg get a whole box of the stuff from their uncle every year—a sort of gift, I guess. They aren't fond of it, so they always give it away freely to anyone they can snag, and I got caught today."

"It smells awful." Jeanne eyed the jar again. "Does anyone really eat that stuff?"

"Sure. It's kind of a Swedish thing, although not all Swedes like it. Everyone who has tried it either loves it or hates it—there's no such thing as middle ground with fermented herring."

Jeanne looked at him. "Have *you* tried it?"

"Of course. I had to see what all the fuss was about."

"And?"

"I hated it. I dumped the rest of it into the dog's dish, but he wouldn't touch it. That's what really made up my mind about fermented herring. If the dog won't even get close to it, then a human has no business eating it."

Jeanne couldn't help but laugh. She felt so much better that she could hardly believe she had been sick a few minutes before. "I guess we should probably head back to town. I've delayed us enough."

"I'm going to hitch up the wagon first."

His tone had shifted, and Jeanne swung her head up to look at him. He wasn't smiling now. In fact, his eyes held almost a betrayed look.

"You need to pick something up in town?" Jeanne tried to keep her voice casual all while her mind raced to figure out what she could have said to set him off.

Ethan shook his head. "I don't need anything from town. I don't think you should be up on horseback."

"But why? I've been doing it every day for two weeks." Jeanne waited, but when he didn't speak immediately, she added. "If you're worried because I got sick, then don't. I'm better now—"

"Jeanne."

He'd never called her by her first name, and it was enough to stop her in her tracks now. She stared at him, watching as his throat bobbed when he swallowed. What was wrong with him?

He met her gaze, his eyes an even darker shade than usual. "You should have told me."

"Told you what?" Maybe she was just dimwitted, but she couldn't for the life of her follow his thinking.

"About the baby."

All at once she understood. At least she thought she understood. Just to make sure, she cautiously asked, "What baby?"

"*Your* baby." Ethan's fingers about strangled his hat—he was gripping it so hard.

"How did you guess?" It was a weak question, but the only thing Jeanne could think to say.

Ethan stared hard at her. "I should have guessed a long time ago, but I wasn't thinking. I *do* know some of the signs. My wife had a baby, in case you forgot."

"Oh." Jeanne wished she could slide right through the floor the way he was looking at her. "I didn't think it would matter if you knew or not."

"Wouldn't matter?" Ethan hardly raised his voice, but the two words held an intensity that sent chills down Jeanne's spine. "Of course, it would have mattered! I would have been more careful, taken a few more precautions—"

He broke off and spun away. Jeanne thought he was going to leave, but he stopped in front of the window, staring outside at nothing.

"Baby," Vivian spoke up, toddling right over and grinning up at him.

"That's right. Mrs. McAllister is going to be a mama, isn't she?"

"Mama?" Vivian cocked her head, testing out the new word.

"Right, a mama." Ethan still wouldn't look at her, but Jeanne caught a tiny tremor in his voice.

"Ethan, I'm sorry," Jeanne blurted out. Only after the words were out did she realize that now *she'd* gone and used *his* given name. Her face heated. "I—um—didn't mean to worry you."

Ethan looked at her, some of the fire in his eyes gone. "Did Pratt know about this?"

Jeanne shook her head. "No one does—except for Sadie and Vivian and now you."

"Well, at least Vivian *tried* to tell me. Now, you and Sadie—" Ethan raked his hand through his hair. "You should have stayed in Columbus."

"Expecting a baby does not make me a china doll." Jeanne had to fight to keep the heat from her words. "In fact, life has been much easier since I came here. Have you ever worked in a hotel? Well, it's not at all glamorous. At least you don't make me empty chamber pots."

"But—" Ethan crushed his hat between his hands again. "Things can go wrong. And I would have felt terrible if something had happened—"

"Ethan Becker, enough. You don't know what you're talking about." Jeanne hopped out of her chair and pushed it back to the table, feeling as if her limbs were coiled springs just waiting to burst free.

Ethan straightened. "I was married. I *do* know what I'm talking about."

"No, you don't. Your wife died in childbirth, and I would guess you know nothing about birth besides that. That experience is all you see when you think of birth, so of course it scares you. And I don't blame you." Jeanne faced him, her irritation with him melting away. How could she stay angry with him when fear lurked in his eyes, making him seem so vulnerable? "You can't let this paralyze you. And I can't let your fear paralyze me either. God is in control, and He will bring this baby in His timing."

Ethan said nothing, just looked at her, and Jeanne took hope. Maybe he would finally be able to stop fretting—although she had to admit that his concern was touching—too much so.

Vivian toddled over to her and grabbed onto her skirt, baby still tucked under her arm. "Baby, feel?"

Jeanne ignored her, focusing instead on Ethan. She refused to be the first to break the stare-down, and he seemed just as determined as her. He shouldn't have been. *She* was the one who was in the right.

Vivian's fist tugged on her skirt again. "Mama, up."

Ethan's eyes went wide and he broke the stare, his gaze flying to Vivian. Without his eyes holding her attention, Vivian's words finally registered in Jeanne's mind, and she gasped. *She didn't just call me "Mama," did she? What a mess!* But it was Ethan's own fault that Vivian was calling her "Mama," so he would have to deal with it.

"Mama," Vivian said again, and Ethan seemed to snap out of his daze.

"No, Vivian, no." He crossed the room and picked her up, his cheeks a shade darker than usual. "Her name is 'Mrs. McAllister,' not 'Mama'—that is, not *your* mama."

"Baby," Vivian sang back at him, grinning. Obviously she thought her papa could use some encouragement from her favorite word.

"Right—she's going to have a baby, and she'll be that baby's mama, but that doesn't make her yours." The more he talked, the redder his face grew. "Can you say 'Mrs. McAllister' instead?"

Vivian bobbed her head. "Mama."

Jeanne had to clap her hand over her mouth to keep from laughing out loud. *McAllister* and *Mama* did have some of the same letters. And *Mama* was a far sight easier for a two-year-old to wrap her tongue around.

Ethan looked stricken, but he heaved a sigh and climbed to his feet. "Guess we'll have to work on that." He clapped his misshapen hat back onto his head and spun toward the door. "I'm going to hitch that wagon up."

Jeanne opened her mouth to speak, but Ethan sent her a look, silencing her. "I know you said that God is in control and He'll bring the baby in His timing, but I see nothing wrong in being a little careful."

He was out the door before she could create a comeback.

Jeanne sighed and dropped back into her seat. Who would have guessed a little jar of fermented herring could cause so much trouble?

10

Judging by the way Jeanne's eyes narrowed when she stepped out of Mayfield Mercantile the next morning, Ethan guessed she had expected a good night's sleep to have cured him of his extra precautions. It hadn't.

In fact, Ethan had spent most of the night trying to find a more comfortable position in his bed as his mind churned out all the "what if" scenarios it could produce. Jeanne's pregnancy bothered him more than he cared to admit to himself. It shouldn't have. She was a healthy woman. She had access to all the nutrition she could need for herself and a growing baby. And she wasn't his to worry about.

Still, knowing the truth had sent his mind on a journey back into the past, a trip he hadn't made in a long time. From all appearances, Mamie had been healthy as well. Ethan had made sure she lacked for nothing. And it still hadn't been enough.

He hated the memory of Mamie's death, hated remembering the helplessness that engulfed him as she lost the fight and her body slowly shut down. There had been nothing he or anyone else could do, but it felt as if there should have been.

Now he watched Jeanne descend the steps, her waist still so slim that he wouldn't have guessed she was carrying a baby, and he had to swallow hard. He liked Jeanne. He wouldn't have thought he could when he first met her two weeks before, but she had grown on him. He wanted her to be healthy and safe—and he was powerless to do anything to keep her that way.

Jeanne stopped in front of him, the highlights in her hair catching the sunlight and making her hair fairly glow. Then Ethan saw her hands on her hips, and he pulled his mind away from pretty highlights. She meant business.

"You're still worrying, aren't you?"

Ethan met her gaze. "Reckon I am."

"Well, don't." And just like that, the lecture was over. She brushed past him and was into the wagon before he could even reach out to help her.

Ethan blew out his breath and climbed up after her. "I might stop worrying if you would take this more seriously."

"I assure you I am very serious." Jeanne set Vivian on her lap, then flicked a comb from her pocket and began running it through Vivian's hair. Ethan hadn't even noticed how tangled her hair was.

Ethan shook his head, then reached under the seat and picked up a jar. "Here," he said, thrusting it at Jeanne. "When you're done with that, drink this."

Jeanne's eyebrows arched. "And what is it?"

"I promise it isn't fermented herring. It's a tea mix that was still in the cupboard from when Mamie was expecting Vivian. She said it always settled her stomach and gave her more energy."

"Oh—well, thank you." Jeanne turned her eyes back to Vivian's hair, her cheeks pinking just a bit. "It was kind of you to think of it."

Little did she know that she was *all* he had been thinking about since yesterday.

Ethan unset the wagon brake and guided the team out of town. Sitting beside Jeanne on the wagon bench would have made talking easier—if he could have thought of anything to say. As it was, he couldn't think of anything she would want to hear, and she didn't seem too inclined to talk either. She just sat there, one arm keeping Vivian in place and the other holding the jar. She didn't seem to have any attention to spare for him—which was just fine. It didn't bother him.

Except that it did—just a little.

"Feels like we might get a storm today," he said, spying the farm up ahead.

"A storm?" Jeanne tilted her face up at the sky. "You're joking."

"Hardly. It's so humid that I bet we'll get a fine thunderstorm later."

"I'll believe it when I see it," Jeanne said, shrugging.

"And how long did you say you've lived in Nebraska?"

"Two years—although I guess that's not entirely accurate because I went east during the first summer to be at my grandma's funeral."

"Exactly." Ethan turned the team into the lane. "We'll see who's right later. But for now, looks like we've made it home."

Jeanne fell quiet, but the moment he reined in the team and set the brake, she was over the edge of the wagon again. Ethan bit back his growl. She was going to break her neck trying to jump down from the wagon with her full skirts and without help.

But there was nothing he could do now except pass Vivian into her waiting arms.

"Guess I'll see you tonight," he said, gathering up the reins.

Jeanne didn't move away immediately. She stood there, looking up at him, and again Ethan couldn't help but notice just what a lovely woman she was.

Jeanne drew in a deep breath. "I'm sorry for all of the misunderstandings that have happened since the time we met. I hope you know that while I was upset with Judge Pratt's verdict, I've tried to be helpful to you while I've been here. Will you forgive me for anything I've done to hurt or annoy you, even if it was unintentional?"

Ethan looked at her, trying to comprehend her apology. Why now, of all times? He thought he had assured her he didn't bear any grudges.

And then he remembered. It was Thursday. Their time was up after today.

The thought nearly knocked the air from his lungs. Over so quickly? What was she going to do after she left? Would she be able to find another job in Columbus? *Should* she find another job with the baby on the way? And yet how could she *not* find another job? She would need money for food and a roof over her head.

He felt paralyzed, his worries for her reaching an all-time crescendo.

"You *do* forgive me, don't you?" Jeanne asked, her forehead furrowed.

Oh, yeah. Her question. Ethan forced a smile to his face. "Of course, I forgive you. And I hope you'll forgive me too. I haven't acted very good during this either, and I'm sure I've hurt and annoyed you as well."

"Good. I'm glad we're cleared on that." Her forehead smoothed and she smiled up at him.

"I guess tomorrow I'll drive you back to Columbus," Ethan said, the words putting a heavy feeling in his middle.

Jeanne's smile dimmed just a bit. "Don't worry about it. I'll take the stage back to Columbus."

Ethan shook his head. "No, I—"

"Yes, I'll take the stage. It's the simplest way, and it will keep you from having to make an unnecessary trip." Jeanne nodded firmly, taking a step back from the wagon. "I'll see you tonight."

Still Ethan hesitated. "I suppose so."

And that would be the last time he saw her. Why did none of this feel right?

11

Jeanne intended to lie down with Vivian only long enough to get the little girl to sleep, but she must have been more tired than she realized. The next time she opened her eyes, the room had darkened.

Careful not to jostle Vivian, Jeanne rolled over and sat up, bending to pull on her boots again. The sky outside the open window had clouded over, but the air still felt too heavy and hot. The curtains hung limply, not stirred by even the faintest breeze.

Jeanne stood, tiptoeing from the bedroom and into the kitchen. Half-peeled potatoes sat on the table, and Jeanne looked from them to the door. Would it be best to finish supper or pull the clothes from the line? As humid as the day had been, the clothes were bound to still be wet, and she hated to spread them all over the kitchen to finish drying. But if it did start raining as Ethan had predicted, then it would do no good to leave them on the line.

A minuscule breeze pushed at the kitchen curtains, and Jeanne thought the wind felt almost cold. She moved for the door. Clothes it would be.

Picking up a basket, Jeanne slipped out the door and hurried down the steps toward the clothesline. She didn't like the feel of the air at all. The clouds above were nearly black, and Jeanne broke into a run.

At the clothesline Jeanne grabbed the clothespins, thrusting them into her apron pocket, and shoved the laundry into the basket. She still had one more line to go when Ethan appeared.

"What are you doing back so early?" Jeanne asked, pushing a sheet into her quickly filling basket.

Ethan pointed at the sky. "Wasn't sure that you would know what to do with a storm like this. It looks like it's going to be a bad one."

The air was still stifling, and Jeanne could feel loose strands of hair sticking to the back of her sweaty neck. "I hope it storms!"

"We could use the rain, but I've a notion that this storm could cause some damage." Ethan grabbed a couple of shirts from the line for her. "I need to put the team away, but I wanted to tell you to close the house up and gather some blankets and a lantern. We'll need to go to the cellar, by my best guess." He dropped the clothes into the basket. "Got it?"

Jeanne nodded but bit her tongue to keep from asking more questions. She didn't know the house had a cellar. And why did he think they would need it? The air was so still that she couldn't imagine it doing any damage.

But Ethan was running back toward the barn, so Jeanne quickened her own pace. Gathering the last of the laundry, she ran to the house and dropped the basket in the kitchen. Then she moved from room to room and shut the windows, latching them closed. By the time she had closed the last of them, a wind was beginning to kick up and the air held a chill. The yard turned dark, and the clouds took on a greenish tint.

Ethan burst into the house just as she had finished gathering the lantern and a stack of quilts. "We better get to the cellar now. Where's Vivian?"

"In her room."

He ran toward the bedroom and returned with Vivian before Jeanne could do more than scoop up her pile of quilts. Ethan grabbed the lantern, then opened the door and motioned for her to follow him.

She stumbled after him, trying to pick up the loose ends of the quilts as she went. Ethan closed the door firmly behind them, then took off down the steps. The wind had turned into a beast during the short time she had been inside. It whipped through the farm, making the grass writhe under its attack, and Jeanne saw a bucket go sailing in front of the barn. This storm was like nothing she had ever seen before. It seemed almost evil, as if it wanted to see them destroyed.

"Hurry!" Ethan yelled over his shoulder, and Jeanne tried to catch up. By the time she reached him, he had set down Vivian and the lantern and was grabbing the handle to a door that led into the ground next to the house.

"What will the animals do?" Jeanne yelled.

"Hopefully they'll be fine!"

"Hopefully?" A scattering of raindrops pelted down from the sky, and Jeanne shivered, rubbing her arms. She thought of Ethan's cows, the horses, the chickens, and especially the new brood of chicks. She hated the thought of them being left out in this storm.

Ethan got the door open and held it against the wind. He spared Jeanne a quick look. "The animals have shelter. They'll be all right."

And he was right—mostly. But the new chicks were still out in the grass behind the coop and were completely exposed to the fury of the storm. "The chicks—"

"I don't care right now." Ethan grabbed Vivian and the lantern, starting down the steps. "Come on!"

Jeanne took a step toward the dark hole leading into the ground, then looked over her shoulder. Ethan might not care about the animals right now—but *she* did. The chicks were too tiny to withstand the storm and would die for sure if they were left alone. The wind was powerful, but she could still fight against it. And it would take only one minute. Just one little minute, and then all those tiny lives would be saved.

"Jeanne!" Ethan called.

She made up her mind. "I'll be right back!" she yelled, throwing her armload of quilts down the steps at him. She took off running, but not fast enough to escape Ethan's voice.

"What? Are you crazy? Get back here, Jeanne—"

The roar of the storm drowned out his voice, and Jeanne shook aside her guilt. He would forgive her when she returned with the chicks.

The wind about knocked her over as she came around the corner of the house, but she regained her balance and pressed onward. Her skirt whipped around her legs, threatening to trip her, and the rain pelted down harder. She reached the barn and paused for just one second, panting. But there was no time to lose. She started forward again, running toward the chicken coop. The chicks were in the grass just behind the coop.

Her foot caught on an uneven spot of ground, and she fell. Breathing hard, she shoved her wet hair back from her face and picked herself up again. She heard the sound of fabric ripping and felt something give at the waist of her dress, but she didn't care. *Just get the chicks, and then get away from this horrible storm.* That was all her mind could process.

From somewhere behind her, Jeanne heard her name, and she risked a backward glance. Ethan was running in her direction, waving her back toward him, but Jeanne shook her head. She'd already come this far, so there was no use turning back now. And what was he thinking leaving Vivian alone in the cellar?

She reached the nest where she and Vivian had watched the chicks play just that afternoon, but a quick scan revealed that it was empty. Empty? Where could they have disappeared to?

"Jeanne, don't!" Ethan called, his voice drawing closer.

He was no doubt furious with her, and Jeanne knew the time had come to give up. The storm was too violent to be out here any longer. She started to turn toward him, but then her eye caught on something in the grass. One chick—its feathers plastered to its small body and lying limp on the ground. She knelt down again, scooping it up and tucking it into her apron pocket.

Ethan yelled something unintelligible, and still cupping the chick with her hand, Jeanne stood. Time to put his worries to rest and get back to the cellar.

All at once pain exploded in her head. She staggered forward, trying to regain her balance, but her own feet tripped her. The world spun. The wind turned into a deafening roar in her ears. Her head felt as if it were about to burst from the sudden pressure that had filled it.

"Jeanne!" Ethan's face hovered in her vision for one second before darkness blotted it out.

Getting her eyes open again proved to be more difficult. Her eyelids didn't seem to want to listen to her, and her first effort failed. She tried again, and this time she caught a glimpse of a too-bright orb of light and Vivian's tearstained face. Pain sliced through her head, and she let her eyes slide shut again, a groan escaping from her lips.

"Mama!" Vivian hiccupped and began to cry, but Jeanne could do nothing to comfort her. She couldn't even help herself.

From somewhere just behind her ear, Ethan made a shushing sound and whispered, "It's all right, Vivie. She'll be fine. Just fine."

Jeanne pried her eyes open again and caught a glimpse of earth walls around her. Where was she? And how had she gotten here?

"Ethan?" Saying his name took more effort than she would have believed possible, and the single word came out more as a groan.

"I'm here." He stirred, and she realized that she was slumped against him, her back to his chest.

Before she could even think to react, he whispered, "Just hold still. Your head is bleeding and I'm trying to get it to stop."

His voice sounded strange, almost shaky, but Jeanne didn't have the energy to ask if he was all right. She didn't even have the energy to ask how he had gotten her into the cellar in the first place.

A shiver wracked her frame, and as another attack of pain gripped her head, she didn't resist as the darkness again washed over her.

Between the darkness and the raindrops coursing down the glass, he could see nothing of the farm, but he didn't care much. Everything inside him seemed numb, in shock—and nothing mattered. Not the farm, the damage from the storm, or even his own damp, mud-streaked clothes—nothing except the small woman he had failed to keep safe.

Closing his eyes, Ethan let his forehead rest against the cold window pane, trying not to think, to remember, to feel. It was no use. He couldn't stop picturing Jeanne's limp form—and he couldn't keep his own terror under control. It threatened to break free and overpower him, cripple him, but he had no time for that. He would be no help to Jeanne if he crumpled.

The door behind him creaked, and he spun around. Florence Hoffman stepped out of the bedroom, and his heart nearly stopped beating.

"Is she worse?" he asked, hardly recognizing his own voice.

Florence lifted her head, closing the door. "Jeanne? No, she isn't worse. Doc Stoning just finished stitching up her head."

Ethan swallowed hard. "It's bad, isn't it?"

"Actually Doc was quite pleased with what he found. She's going to have a raging headache for a while, but Doc is sure she'll make a full recovery."

"Thank God." Ethan closed his eyes, then opened them just as fast. "The baby? Will it—is it going to be—fine?"

"Doc thinks so." Florence moved to the stove and pulled a pot of water onto the burner. "It's good that you got the cut on Jeanne's head to stop bleeding. Head wounds can bleed a lot."

"It was the least I could do." Ethan couldn't keep the bitterness from his voice. "It was about *all* I could do. You'll never know how many times I second-guessed my own judgment in waiting out the storm in the cellar rather than riding for Doc right away."

"You did the right thing. You would have been no help to Jeanne if you had got yourself killed riding out in a storm like that. And you were wise to come to me first so that Jeanne wouldn't be alone for very long." Florence left the stove and patted his arm. "There's nothing you could have done better."

"Except maybe kept her safe in the first place?" Ethan pulled his arm away from her. "She was trying to save some chicks, Florence. Nothing more than a few *chicks.*"

"She's very softhearted."

"Well, it about got her killed this time. It was a piece of the chicken coop that hit her. I saw it coming, and I tried to call to her, but the crazy lady stood right up and got hit in the back of the head." Ethan rubbed at his forehead. "She's always getting into scrapes."

"At least you were looking out for her."

"I tried, but obviously it wasn't enough." Ethan heaved a sigh. "Still, I'm even more afraid of what she's going to do to herself after she goes back to Columbus. Her two weeks ended today."

"I thought you were looking forward to getting her off your hands."

"I was." Ethan frowned down at a crack in the floor. "I was. But now I'm just worried about her."

"Then maybe you should ask her to stay," Florence suggested.

"Stay?" Ethan snorted a laugh. "What could I offer her that would make her want to stay?"

"Oh, you have plenty you could offer her. Security. A home. A family."

Ethan snapped his head up to look at her. "Oh, no, you don't. I'm not in love with Jeanne."

"I'm sorry." Florence delicately lifted her hand to her mouth. "It's just that you seem so concerned about every part of her life that I thought you must care for her."

"I *do* care about her. So does Vivian."

"Ah, yes. Enough that she calls her 'Mama,' right?"

Ethan glared at her. "That was a mistake. I don't know how to break her of the habit."

"Maybe you shouldn't try. Maybe you should listen to your two-year-old and do some real soul-searching. Perhaps Vivian has a better sense of how things are than you do."

"That's ridiculous." Ethan glanced at her, hoping she was joking. She looked serious.

"I like Jeanne—don't get me wrong," he said, trying again. "I think she's a special little lady, and I hope some man sees her value and gives her the home and family she deserves, but I—well, I'm hardly in a position to be that man."

"And why is that?" Florence asked. She didn't seem inclined to let him off the hook.

"Because—" Ethan stopped, trying to sort out his thoughts. "Because—"

Florence's eyebrows rose. "Because if you let yourself love her, you might lose her—is that it? She does have the life-threatening condition of expecting a baby."

Ethan's face heated. "That's not fair."

"You seemed to be struggling to find the words, so I was only trying to help. Do you have a better explanation?"

Ethan could think of nothing to say, and the longer silence stretched, the more her words condemned him.

"All right," he said at last. "Maybe you're right. I just can't forget what happened to Mamie."

Florence reached out to touch his arm again, and this time Ethan didn't flinch away. "You had a bad time of it, Ethan, and I understand your fears. But women have babies every day, and most births have no complications. I had four boys and never had any trouble. But even if Jeanne did have complications, do you suppose you'd be able to keep yourself from hurting by not marrying her?"

Ethan looked down at the floor, and Florence added, "Holding Jeanne at arm's length isn't going to protect you. I think you already care more than you realize, and instead of keeping yourself safe, letting her get away from you is going to smash something precious."

Ethan could hear his heart hammering in his ears, but before he could speak, the bedroom door opened again. Ethan jerked his head around and watched Doc Stoning enter the room.

"There's nothing more I can do here, so I'm going home," Doc said, reaching for his rain slicker. He looked at Florence. "You'll stay?"

Florence nodded. "Ethan already told Sadie what happened so that she wouldn't be worried when Jeanne didn't come home, and I'm sure she'll be organizing the other women to spell me off in the morning, if I don't miss my guess."

Ethan's face must have reflected his confusion, because Doc Stoning said, "I'm afraid Mrs. McAllister is going to have to stay here for now. She seems stabilized enough, but I don't want to move her for at least a few days."

"And, of course, you'll need to be chaperoned for propriety's sake," Florence added. "We wouldn't want to start tongues to talking."

Ethan felt his face heat. "Oh, of course."

Then Florence leaned closer. "But if you want your home's privacy back, you could marry her."

"Ha," was all Ethan would give her. But he began working the suggestion in his mind—and neither gossips nor propriety had anything to do with it.

12

Jeanne stared up at the ceiling, the quilt tucked snugly against her chin and the room completely quiet. Her head ached, but not too badly if she laid still. And lying still was about all she could do right now. She couldn't even read the books or copies of the *Osceola Record* that one of the women had left beside her bed.

Of all the stupid things she had ever done, this had to top it off. Ethan must be furious with her. First she had ignored his warnings and run into the storm—to save a flock of chicks that she hadn't ended up being able to save. And then she had gotten herself hurt, and now she had overtaken his room and inconvenienced him. He had called her troublesome when he first brought her here. She hated to think of what he must be calling her now that she had completely disrupted his home and schedule.

And, of course, it always came down to a case of never thinking before acting. All her efforts to be helpful to him invariably spun out of control.

Voices murmured outside her door, and Jeanne strained to listen. She was able to pick out one voice, Mrs. Holling's, the woman who was on duty for the "chaperoning" today. Then a male voice caught her attention, and her heart picked up speed in spite of herself. Ethan must be home.

Even though she knew how upset he must be with her, Jeanne couldn't stop the warm feeling that spread through her middle. She liked having him nearby. And it really had been gallant of him to come after her and rescue her in spite of her stupidity.

"I just don't know if I should let you." Mrs. Holling's voice quavered outside the door.

"I don't see how there's anything improper about it," Ethan's voice replied. "I know you're just trying to protect her, but I'm not going to hurt her."

"Oh, Ethan, of course I don't think you would ever hurt Mrs. McAllister. That's not my reasoning at all. I just don't know if it would be proper—and that's why I'm here. To make sure things are *proper.*"

"I understand, and I want things to be proper as well. But we'll keep the door wide open, and you'll be here to make sure nothing untoward happens."

"But when I came to spell off Mrs. Durmond this morning, she was quite strict with me about how we should keep things *proper*—"

"Oh, I'm sure she was." Jeanne heard the floorboards shift, and Ethan's voice came closer. "Could I just ask Mrs. McAllister—?"

"Oh, no. She must rest, and we can't be disturbing her."

Jeanne had endured enough. "Mrs. Holling!" she called, then grabbed the sides of her head at the pain that exploded. Yelling wasn't such a good idea after all.

The door creaked open, and Mrs. Holling's plump face appeared. "Did you say something, dear?"

"Yes. Let Ethan in." Jeanne forced her hands away from her head and even managed a smile. "Could you help me sit up?"

Mrs. Holling frowned but stepped into the room to slide another pillow under Jeanne's head. "Are you sure, dear? We don't want to hurt your reputation."

"I'm not concerned about that. As Ethan said, we'll leave the door open, and you'll be here as well," Jeanne said, pulling the covers up higher.

"If you're sure." Mrs. Holling bustled back toward the door, and Jeanne lifted her hand to her hair. Not that it did much good. Between the bandage wrapped around her head and the tangled clumps her hair hung in, she knew she was a mess.

Mrs. Holling allowed Ethan through the door, and Jeanne found herself unable to look up at him. She looked awful. She had infuriated him—inconvenienced him—imposed on his life. How much worse could it get?

He stopped beside her bed, and with his voice little more than a whisper, he said, "I have something for you."

Something soft and fuzzy touched her hand, and Jeanne shifted her gaze from the quilt to her hand. "A chick?" Her fingers closed around it, and Ethan released it.

"The chick you found during the storm didn't make it, but yesterday morning the broody hen showed up with all the other chicks in company. They all seemed to have weathered the storm just fine."

"But how?" Jeanne kept her eyes fixed on the chick, one finger stroking its yellow head.

"I guess the broody hen knew to find better shelter, although I'm not sure just where she went. Animals are smart like that sometimes."

Jeanne swallowed. He was acting so nicely that she felt like sinking right through the mattress and hiding under the bed after all she had done. "I should have listened to you."

He didn't have to ask what she was talking about. "You should have," he agreed, but his voice was still gentle.

"I suppose you're pretty mad at me."

"Mad? No, I'm not mad at you."

"But—but I've caused so much trouble." Tears sprang into her eyes without her bidding, and she tried to fight them back.

Ethan seemed to think through his response. "I guess I was mad with you at first—but only because I was afraid for you. Until you've experienced a Nebraska storm, you can't imagine how quickly it can turn violent. I knew what could happen, and it frustrated me that you wouldn't listen. But after you actually got hurt—"

He stopped, and Jeanne dared to lift her eyes to his. He met her gaze, his eyes filled with emotions she didn't even want to begin guessing at. "After you got hurt, I was terrified, and I could feel nothing except that."

Jeanne looked down, unable to hold his gaze any longer. The silence that settled between them threatened to become awkward, and almost in spite of herself, Jeanne said, "I'm sorry for all the extra work I've caused you . . . and for taking over your house . . . and your room—" She thought she had banished her tears, but now they again pressed at her eyes, fighting to spring free. Wretched emotions.

"It's all right," Ethan said comfortably. "Sleeping on the floor isn't doing me too much harm."

"The floor?" It was worse than she thought. "Why can't you sleep with Vivian?"

"I *am* sleeping with Vivian. She's on the floor with me."

"But why—?"

"Our chaperone needs a bed too. She has Vivian's bed, and Vivian and I moved into the parlor for now."

This was terrible. Just terrible. Jeanne tried to sniff back her tears, but it was no use. First one and then another slid down her cheeks.

"Jeanne?" Ethan crouched down, tilting his head to look into her eyes. "Jeanne, why are you crying?"

"You're—sleeping on the—floor?"

"Yes."

"On the—floor?"

"What's so bad about the floor?" Without giving her a chance to respond, Ethan thrust a handkerchief in front of her. "Here—now stop crying. You shouldn't be getting all upset."

Jeanne accepted the handkerchief and wiped at her nose. "It's just—I've caused you so much trouble."

"So?"

"And you were supposed to be able to get rid of me on Thursday."

Ethan stared at her as if she had spouted Chinese. "Get rid of you?"

"You know. My two weeks were over and I was going to return to Columbus."

"Oh, yes—that." Ethan frowned down at the chick still cupped in her hand. "I hardly call that 'getting rid' of you."

"Well, then what *do* you call it?" Jeanne asked, although she wasn't sure she really wanted to know his answer.

"I call it more of a case of *letting* you get away." Ethan gave her a long look. "And given the way things are, I guess you won't be doing that anytime soon."

Jeanne's heart about stopped. What was he saying? It sounded nothing like the Ethan Becker she knew.

Their gazes locked, and Jeanne found herself unable to catch her breath. This made no sense. What was happening to her? What was happening to *them*?

"Okay, I figure you've probably been visiting long enough." Mrs. Holling's voice quavered from the doorway.

Ethan was the first to look away. His eyes traveled to Mrs. Holling, then back to Jeanne. "I better go—before I get in trouble."

Jeanne smiled, but the effort felt a bit lopsided. "I'm glad you came."

Ethan leaned a bit closer, taking the chick from her hands. "It was a chore," he muttered. "They blocked me out yesterday morning . . . and in the evening when I got home . . . and this morning. I was about to try climbing through the window."

Jeanne lifted her gaze to his face and again collided with his warm, dark eyes. "But—but why? Why go to so much effort to see me?"

"Well, I like you, Jeanne. That's why."

He hesitated for one brief second, and Jeanne felt it only fair that she say, "I like you too, Ethan."

And how had they gotten to this point of calling each other by their first names? It was just one more of those troublesome ties that seemed to be binding them closer together all the time.

13

"What do you think you're doing?"

In one sweep of his gaze, Ethan sized up the situation and crossed the dining room in three strides, not waiting for Jeanne to respond. Snatching the broom out of her hands, he pointed a finger at the nearest chair. "Sit. You're hardly supposed to be out of bed, let alone cleaning my house."

Jeanne didn't move, just looked back at him with her prettiest and most coaxing smile. "I feel good, and I *was* taking it easy."

Ethan narrowed his eyes at her. "And where are all the women who are supposed to be watching over you?"

"Florence was here, but I told her to go home. I don't need a nurse, and I'm capable of knowing when I need to rest."

Ethan pointed at the chair again. "*Sit* down."

Jeanne eyed him for a moment, then sighed and lowered herself into the chair. "You don't give me enough credit. I *am* being careful, but I need to be busy. It's been over a week since I got hurt, and I've felt like such a burden."

"Then take up knitting, or crocheting, or—or quilting."

The look on her face told him she wasn't going for that one.

"Has anyone ever mentioned that you worry too much?" Jeanne asked, folding her arms.

"Has anyone ever told you that you ought to take more care with yourself?" Ethan asked, folding his arms as well.

Jeanne heaved another longsuffering sigh. "I don't understand why you have to be so fussy. I was getting along just fine without you a month ago."

Everything Ethan intended to say slid straight from his mind. So she had noticed that he was acting a bit protective of her. He wanted her safe. He wanted her happy. And most shocking of all, he wanted her to stay. Forever. He wanted her to be his.

None of the emotions he had been dealing with since her accident felt familiar. He still hadn't made heads or tails of most of them, but the more days passed, the more visits he paid Jeanne; and the more he tried to create ways to cheer her up, the surer he became of one thing—Florence was entirely right. Something precious was being created between them, and letting her get away was becoming less of an option with every passing day.

Jeanne wasn't Mamie. Jeanne was alive and vibrant, glowing with enthusiasm and a love for others around her.

How was it that just four weeks ago he hadn't known of her existence? How had he managed to get along without her caring for Vivian, taking him to task for the lack of cleanliness in his house, brightening his day with her smile and laugh?

She liked him. She had told him that much. But how deep did that liking go? Was it as deep as his was for her? Did it go so deep that it turned into—love?

"I'm sorry," Jeanne said, breaking through his thoughts.

He looked up and saw the regret on her face. "Sorry?" he repeated.

"I didn't mean to hurt your feelings with what I just said. I'm always speaking without thinking. You aren't *that* fussy. Just enough that it sometimes steps on my nerves."

Ethan hid his smile. "You didn't hurt my feelings. I simply got to thinking about something else."

"Oh?" Jeanne raised one eyebrow at him.

"I've been thinking," Ethan said slowly, trying to sort out his thoughts as he spoke. "And I wondered if you like it here."

Jeanne blinked. "Like it here? Well, of course I do. I can't remember the last time I've felt so at home or happy as I do here."

She bit her lip as if she had said too much, but Ethan felt his heart expand until it nearly pressed against his chest. It was better than he had hoped for.

Schooling his features into what he hoped was a stoic expression, he said, "I've been thinking about that bargain we made."

Jeanne frowned, but then her forehead cleared. "Oh, you mean Judge Pratt's bargain."

"Yes, that one. It seems to have worked well, don't you think? I haven't had to worry about Vivian or the house and extra chores, and you've had all your needs met."

"I suppose." Jeanne's eyes studied him.

"Well, your time is up and your fine has been taken care of, but I sort of like the arrangement we've come to." Ethan drew in a breath, aware that his palms were growing sweaty. "What if we were to keep working together? Not much would change, but now I would be—" He nearly slipped up and said *courting you*, but he caught himself and choked out the words "—paying you."

Jeanne's eyes widened. "You think it would work?"

Ethan heard the interest in her voice, and it was all he could do to keep his voice steady as he said, "Yes, I see no reason that it shouldn't."

Jeanne tilted her head. "It doesn't seem fair for me to keep imposing on the Mayfields."

"Maybe you could talk with them about paying rent now that I'll be paying you." And if all went well, she wouldn't be with the Mayfields for much longer. If his plan worked, their courtship should be ended within a couple more months and she would become his wife.

But if it didn't work—

Ethan frowned. He didn't want to think of it. All he could do was focus on one step at a time, and for right now, that step was to get Jeanne to agree to stay in Osceola rather than returning to Columbus.

He took a peek at Jeanne's face and found himself unable to judge what she thought of his idea. She had seemed excited at first, but now her face had clouded. His chest tightened. What if she turned his offer down? What if she didn't want to be a part of his life anymore, not even as simple a part as being his employee? Was there even a chance he could change her mind if that were the case?

At last Jeanne looked up. "I'll think about what you've said."

She sounded so formal that he would have laughed if there hadn't been so much that hinged on her decision. He didn't want her to *think* about it. He wanted her to give him an enthusiastic yes that would prove that she had meant it when she said she liked him.

Doubt began to crowd its way into his mind, and the plan that had seemed so perfect when he woke up this morning suddenly seemed full of holes. Just one *no* from her, and his dreams would be destroyed—along with his heart.

Because his heart was very much tied into this. Somehow in between hitting heads with her in the Columbus Hotel and watching her run away from him into the storm, Jeanne McAllister had captured his heart without his even realizing it.

14

It was incredible how she could feel so part of this community after being here for only four Sundays—especially since she hadn't been very impressed with Osceola at first.

Holding Vivian, Jeanne smiled and greeted the women who passed her, lunch baskets on their arms. After Pastor Drew's sermon, nearly all of the congregation had gathered on the bank of Davis Creek, which now held only a little water from the last storm but still made a nice picnicking spot. Of course, a few trees would have made it perfect, but trees were a rarity around here. It made her all the more appreciative of the hard work Ethan had gone to in getting trees started around the house. Someday they would appreciate the shade and fruit the trees produced.

He *will appreciate it, silly. There's no* you *included in it.*

Somehow the thought did nothing to diminish the glow inside her. But then, maybe that had something to do with the fact that she had just caught sight of Ethan coming her way, bearing the basket she had prepared for them at the Mayfields' that morning. He had been the one who suggested she make up a basket for them when he mentioned the picnic yesterday. Just for him and Vivian and her.

"I took a peek on my way over," Ethan said, giving the basket a pat as he drew closer to her. "I love your ham sandwiches and cinnamon rolls."

She knew—that was why she had made them. But rather than telling him that, she just smiled and took the basket from him. Setting it onto the ground with Vivian, she pulled out the blanket on top and snapped it open. Ethan caught the other end and helped her lay it flat on the ground.

Their eyes met, and Ethan flashed her a smile. Her cheeks heated, and quickly she turned to grab the basket.

When she turned back, Ethan had already sat down and Vivian was climbing into his lap. Lowering herself to the ground, Jeanne placed the basket in the center of the blanket and set to work pulling out the food and dishes. She glanced at Ethan one more time and caught him watching her. That only made her heart race all the more.

"So," Ethan said, not sounding at all uncomfortable, "have you considered what we talked about?"

Keeping her gaze on the food, Jeanne asked, "And what would that be?"

"About staying on and letting me hire you?"

"Oh." Jeanne felt her heart sink. "Um, no—I haven't given it too much thought yet. I'm sure you'd like a decision, of course—"

She let her voice trail off and risked another glance at him. His eyes had darkened, but when their gazes met, he smiled—a bit forced.

"Take all the time you need. I'm not in a hurry." He waited as she passed him a plate, then asked, "Are you busy this afternoon?"

"Busy?" Jeanne looked around them at the other families and couples.

"I meant after the picnic."

"I suppose not." She had thought she might take a nap when she got back to the Mayfields', but something in his eyes kept her from mentioning that.

"Well, if you aren't busy, then maybe you'd want to take a little drive with me and Vivian? It's a nice afternoon and it seems a shame not to use it."

A drive? Jeanne was sure her eyes must be round. She had never gone on a drive for no reason other than enjoying the afternoon—or the company.

"Ah—well, I guess that sounds fun," she said, not giving herself time to try to read the intentions behind his offer. He was probably just being nice.

But the smile that lit up his face made her question if it was really just niceness that compelled his offer—or something else that she didn't even dare consider.

Even if she did return to Columbus, Jeanne knew she would never, ever forget this day. It was the kind that would never repeat itself, but for as long as it lasted, she would treasure every moment of it. First a church service spent sitting at Ethan's side, and then a picnic with him, and now a drive. It was nearly too much to take in.

When he had mentioned a drive, she had imagined a ride much like the one they made every morning and evening between Osceola and the farm. She hadn't expected Ethan to forego the heavy-framed farm wagon and instead rent a buggy from the livery, but that was exactly what he had done. And when she had commented that he didn't need to do that, he just smiled into her eyes and said he wanted to.

Why was he going to the extra trouble and expense? Was he trying to make her feel special—or was her mind spinning ideas because she *wanted* to imagine that he thought she was special?

Of course you're only imagining it. Ethan has nothing but business in mind when he looks at you.

Only—he didn't seem to have business on his mind this afternoon. Apart from his single question at lunch about whether or not she had made a decision, he hadn't mentioned anything related to work. He kept the conversation light, telling her about his past and asking questions about hers, listening to her responses as if everything she said really mattered to him.

He made it easy for her imagination to work overtime—and that encouragement was the last thing she needed. Ethan didn't have a permanent position in her life, and pretending that he did would only lead to devastating results when they parted ways.

And *that* was why she debated over letting him hire her. She wanted to say yes to his offer—she would have given anything to keep him in her life. But someday there would come a point when he no longer needed her, and then her departure would only be that much more heart-shattering.

"Are you all right?" Ethan asked, and Jeanne realized that they were drawing close to Osceola again.

She dipped her head in a nod. "Yes, I—I'm fine."

She could feel his eyes on her, studying her, but he said nothing more until he drew the team to a stop in front of Mayfield Mercantile.

"We should do this again sometime."

Again? Jeanne's heart pounded faster. She wanted to agree—being with Ethan made her happy. Well, maybe *happy* was an understatement. Perhaps *blissful,* or *delirious with joy,* or *nearly touching heaven* would have been more accurate.

Her *yes* was on the tip of her tongue, but just in time, she caught herself and bit down on her lip. No! Her heart was already too tied up in this strange friendship they had formed, and spending any unnecessary time with him was just asking for trouble.

"Jeanne?" Ethan leaned forward, inserting himself into her vision, and Jeanne knew she had to get away before she agreed to things she would one day regret.

"I'll think about it," she said, the answer sliding easily off her tongue. Not a flat out no—but definitely not an agreement. Because she never would do this again.

Ethan frowned a bit. "Jeanne, are you—?"

"My! Would you look at how late it's getting!" Jeanne looked away from him, pretending that the sun's position suddenly held great interest. In reality, it didn't even register with her. "I need to be getting inside before Ephraim and Sadie come looking for me." No way could she let him start asking questions—she had always been too honest for her own good, and he would be sure to see all the emotions churning their way through her.

Ethan's frown deepened, but as he opened his mouth, Jeanne nearly shoved Vivian into his arms. She was down from the buggy in one hop. "Thank you very much for the ride!" she called over her shoulder.

"Wait!" Ethan called, but Jeanne flew past the store's display window and around the corner toward the Mayfields' living quarters. Her heart raced. *Fool! Now he knows that something set you off, and he'll be asking about it tomorrow. He's just persistent enough that he's bound to get the truth out of you—that you care too much about him.*

She half feared Ethan might come after her now, but evidently a team of horses and his two-year-old daughter were all he could manage at the moment, because he didn't appear.

And besides, he was probably thinking exactly what she was— he could catch her tomorrow and force the truth out of her then.

Jeanne rubbed her hand across her face, aware that she was trembling. What was she going to do about this? She hadn't thought she cared this deeply for him, but a little encouragement from him had her dreaming for the moon. He was going to guess how she felt about him—but how could she keep him from knowing?

Get away. The answer was almost audible, and Jeanne latched onto it. Yes, she had to get away as fast as she could. Preferably before she had to see him tomorrow and explain why she was leaving.

But how could she do that? The stage would leave town midmorning, and Ethan would arrive long before that. The liveryman would never let her take her horse out by herself—Ethan had never revoked his order that he alone could commission her use of the horse. There seemed to be no good way out.

Jeanne closed her eyes, drawing in a deep breath. *Lord, what would You have me do? Everything seems to be a mess right now, and*

I'm afraid to think of staying and just as afraid to think of going.
Please, can You make a way for me and provide for my needs? Show
me what You would have me do.

Slowly, her feet dragging, Jeanne made her way to the door
and slipped inside. Maybe if she slept on the question she would
be able to come up with another solution—or maybe the courage
to face Ethan and tell him herself that she was leaving.

Voices murmured from the Mayfields' kitchen, and not eager
to face the family, Jeanne tiptoed down the narrow hall leading to
the room she shared with little Margie and Christina. She wished
she could skip supper entirely, but she knew better than that.
Having an empty stomach was a good way to bring back her
nausea, so she would have to visit the kitchen eventually. But not
until she had had some time alone to quiet her raging emotions.

Just before she closed the bedroom door, she heard Ephraim
say something about Columbus. She froze, straining to hear more
and focused on picking out Ephraim's deep voice from the clatter
of pots and the giggles from the children.

"—hate the thought of making such a long trip away from
you, but who knows when Bert will feel up to driving again, and
all the other freighters are booked tight. 'Fraid I don't have much
choice—be back as soon as possible, of course, but it will still be a
couple days' round trip—planning to leave tomorrow before the
sun's even up, just so I'll be home that much quicker—"

Jeanne's breath caught. Was he saying what she thought he
was? Could this be the answer she was looking for?

Ephraim's voice moved a bit closer. "If you need anything
special from Columbus, just add it to the list and I'll see if I can
get it. But don't make the list *too* long, because you know that the

longer I have to spend shopping, the longer it'll take me to get home."

Sadie made some quip in response, but Jeanne didn't hear it. So Ephraim was going to Columbus tomorrow—and before the sun even rose.

Jeanne crept back to her room and softly shut the door. She leaned against it, closing her eyes as tears pricked against them. She couldn't have asked for a clearer answer—but it was going to tear her heart up. Hopefully Ethan and Vivian wouldn't mind too much when they realized she had left without telling them good-bye, but there was no earthly way she could make herself do that. It would be better this way. Ethan would learn to get along without her again, and Vivian would forget about her before long.

If only she could do the same.

15

"**A**re you sure about this?"

Sadie must have asked the question at least half a dozen times already, enough that it would have annoyed Jeanne if she hadn't known the care that lay behind it. As it was, the question only made her all the more aware of the friends she was leaving behind—and the uncertain future she was running toward.

Picking up the last of her bags, Jeanne offered Sadie what she hoped would pass as a smile. "I'm sure. I've thought about this for a long time."

"But Ephraim made his decision to go to Columbus only last night."

Jeanne shrugged. "Well, I've thought about this long enough. Please. Don't worry about me."

Sadie nibbled on her lower lip, but she said nothing as they walked toward the team standing with their heads hanging low in the yellow light streaming from the kitchen window.

"Maybe you can visit us again someday," Sadie said, stepping to the side. "There's talk that the railroad may bring a line through

Osceola sometime in the next year. Maybe you could plan a trip after the baby arrives."

"Maybe." Jeanne couldn't find the heart to tell Sadie that railroad or not, there would be no return visit. She wouldn't be able to stand seeing Ethan and Vivian again.

Ephraim materialized out of the darkness beside the wagon. "Ready?"

Jeanne nodded and let him take her bag from her. She turned to Sadie. "I guess this is goodbye."

Sadie's nose wrinkled. "Goodness—I'm going to cry."

"Don't. Please." Jeanne was sure she had dried up all her tears the night before as she cried into her pillow, but if Sadie started up, she couldn't be sure of how she would react.

Sadie blinked, brushed at the corners of her eyes, then blinked again and gave a loud sniff. "I'll miss you."

"And I'll miss you too." Jeanne accepted Sadie's hug, then stepped back with a sigh. "Thank you for all you've done for me."

Sadie waved her hand. "I've hardly done a thing."

"Well, I appreciate it all the same."

Jeanne turned to climb into the wagon, but Sadie's voice stopped her. "Jeanne? You and Ethan didn't fight, did you?"

Jeanne swung around. "No, not all. What would make you think that?"

Sadie shrugged. "Just wondered."

"No, Ethan—well, he is—you see—he—" Jeanne found herself unable to continue. She couldn't honestly say that he had agreed with her leaving. Nor could she say he approved of it. Instead, she turned back to the wagon and accepted Ephraim's hand up.

She looked away as Ephraim and Sadie embraced and exchanged their goodbyes. Her eyes burned. Ethan wouldn't even be awake yet. How would he react when he realized she was gone? Would he be frustrated that she hadn't had the nerve to tell him that she didn't want him to hire her?

The wagon shifted as Ephraim climbed up, and he gathered the reins, clucking to the horses. The team lurched forward, and Jeanne waved to Sadie. Then she dug into her pocket and pulled out her handkerchief, blowing her nose. Her nose might run, but she would not cry. It would solve nothing.

The harness jingled and the horses' hooves made a soft thudding sound as they pulled the wagon through the sleeping town. Jeanne watched the houses slide by, their windows dark and the curtains drawn. She almost felt like a runaway.

They passed the livery, and Jeanne stared at the barred door, her mind flashing back to the day the liveryman had blocked her from her horse. Ethan had warned her against trying to outrun him, telling her that whether she tried to escape on foot or by horse, he would catch her.

Jeanne resisted the urge to look over her shoulder. He had no right to come after her now that she had "paid" her fine. He had no *reason* to come after her—but she wished he did.

Jeanne shook her head, trying to dispel her thoughts of that man. She gave the livery one final glance. Too bad she couldn't take her horse with her and save Ethan the hassle of finding someone to return it to the Columbus livery. Oh, well. That was what Ethan got for banning her from her horse.

Jeanne slumped back on her seat. This was going to be a long ride if she couldn't stop thinking of him.

At first Ethan figured Jeanne must be delayed. He fidgeted with the reins, scolded Vivian when she wiggled to get down from the wagon seat, and tipped his head back to look at the sun. Something had to be wrong. Usually she was waiting for him on the Mayfield Mercantile steps, and it wasn't like her to be this late.

Climbing down from the wagon, Ethan swung Vivian to his hip and tied the team to the hitching rail. He started up the steps but stopped when he saw the "Closed" sign. Closed on a Monday morning? What was going on here?

Ethan headed for the Mayfields' living quarters, his pace faster than normal and making Vivian giggle. He stopped at the door and rapped. No one came immediately, so he knocked again, a little louder this time.

The door swung open before he could begin a third round of pounding, and Sadie smiled in greeting. "Ethan, what brings you here today?"

"I saw the store was closed." Not his number-one concern at the moment, but he owed it to Sadie at least to act politely. "Is Ephraim all right?"

"Ephraim? Oh, he's fine. Our usual freighter is down ill, so Ephraim went to fetch some supplies for the store." Sadie opened the door wider. "Would you like to come in and have some coffee?"

Ethan shook his head. "No, thank you. Is Jeanne all right?"

"Jeanne? I think it was a difficult morning for her, but that's to be expected. She held up well. I'm going to miss her."

"Miss her?" Ethan narrowed his eyes. What nonsense was Sadie spouting off now?

Sadie just looked at him, her eyebrows arched. "She *did* tell you, didn't she?"

"Tell me what?" Ethan waited for her to continue but she didn't. She just stood there watching him.

"Sadie." He let a note of warning edge his voice. "Where is Jeanne?"

"She's gone."

"Gone?"

"To Columbus."

"Columbus?" The word turned into more of a yell. "What are you talking about? Jeanne has no business going to Columbus!"

Sadie shook her head. "I wondered if she had told you."

Ethan turned away, raking his hand through his hair, then spun back to face Sadie. "When?"

"She left this morning."

"This is insanity!" He was yelling again, and he made himself lower his voice. "Why? Why would she do such a crazy thing as that?"

Sadie shrugged. "Your guess is as good as mine. Better, probably. You spent all day with her yesterday. Didn't she mention it then?"

"No." Ethan scrubbed his hand through his hair again. "She didn't say a word about it. In fact, I thought she was going to agree to stay on here in Osceola and let me hire her. But this—this is ridiculous. Just ridiculous."

"I'm sorry, Ethan, but I guess there's nothing to be done now."

Ethan lifted his head and stared at her. "Nothing to be done? Of *course* there's something to be done! I'm going after her."

"What?" Now it was Sadie's turn to stare. "But you can't—"

"Sure I can. Now, will you watch Vivian while I'm gone?" Ethan thrust Vivian toward her, but Sadie stepped back.

"Ethan, you aren't thinking clearly."

"Jeanne's the one who isn't thinking clearly. Columbus holds nothing good for her, and I'm going to make her get back here until she sees the light."

"But you can't do that. You can't *make* her do anything, Ethan."

"We'll see." He held Vivian out to her again. "Please. This has already wasted too much time. I have to at least try, Sadie. You understand, don't you?"

Sadie accepted Vivian but shook her head. "No, I'm afraid I don't understand. What is going after her really going to gain you? You know I'm here if you need help—"

"Help?" Ethan stared back at her. "This has nothing to do with hiring Jeanne. I'm going to get down on my knees and beg that woman to marry me."

Sadie's eyebrows shot upward. "Marry you? Why?"

"Because I'm crazy in love with her—that's why. Have been for a while now."

"Oh, Ethan!" Sadie let out a squeal and clapped. "That's the best news this little town has ever seen! I thought you'd never come around."

"Well, I'm not the stubborn one right now, but I'll get that little lady to come around too."

Ethan took off running and Sadie called, "How are you going to catch up to her?"

"Never underestimate a lawman!" Ethan yelled back.

16

The sun was too hot. The edge of the seat dug into her legs. The breeze tormented her hat. And her nose wouldn't stop running.

"Look," Ephraim said after yet another round of nose-blowing. "There's no need to cry. If you really don't want to go to Columbus, then just return home with me. Sadie will be glad to let you stay on with us."

Jeanne whisked her handkerchief back into her pocket. "I'm not crying."

Ephraim looked askance at her, and Jeanne stiffened her spine. "My nose is runny—that's all. I *want* to go to Columbus—and I'm not changing my mind."

Ephraim shrugged. "Have it your way. Just hope you don't wipe your nose clean off your face before we get there."

Jeanne refrained from commenting and looked away, clamping her arms against her middle. She felt the baby move, as if in protest, and she couldn't keep from smiling. Too bad Vivian wasn't here. She would be delighted to finally feel some movement.

But she wasn't.

Jeanne's smile died and her nose began to run again, sending her reaching for her handkerchief once more.

The pounding of hooves on the path behind them warned her that a rider was approaching, and swiping her handkerchief under her nose one more time, Jeanne whisked it out of sight. Sniffling in front of Ephraim was bad enough—there was no need for yet another man to be clued in on her emotional state. Ephraim shifted on the bench beside her, looking back, and Jeanne realized that whoever was coming up behind them was riding awfully fast. Maybe her red nose wasn't the biggest of her concerns after all.

She twisted around on her seat just as the rider yelled, "Hold up!"

And then she stared. Surely it couldn't be—no, Ethan wouldn't come after her. Not just to say goodbye.

Ephraim pulled back on the reins, and the wagon ground to a stop. The horse and rider closed the gap between them with alarming speed. Jeanne watched, unable to tear her gaze away as the horse—her horse from the Columbus livery—drew even to the wagon and stopped, sides heaving. The man jumped to the ground, and as his eyes swiveled to meet hers, any trace of doubt disappeared. Ethan *had* come after her.

He pointed at her. "You had no right to do that to me!"

His eyes burned into hers, and Jeanne's heart nearly stopped beating. "Do wh-what to you?"

"You left without even telling me you were leaving."

Jeanne's eyes dropped. "But I paid my fine, so I didn't think it would matter if I left without talking to you."

"Of course it mattered!"

"Well, I—I'm sorry. Was there any paperwork I needed to fill out?"

"Depends." Ethan eyed her. "I need you to come back to Osceola, and if you need an excuse, I could make one."

Jeanne shook her head. "You aren't making any sense."

"Well, then—let me explain." Ethan took a step closer, bringing his horse with him. "I've had some time to think on the ride here, and I decided you must have one of three reasons for leaving."

"One of—three?" Jeanne felt her mouth go dry. He had been analyzing why she left?

"Of course. You had to have a reason for turning down my offer of a job you admitted you enjoyed and instead going in search of a job like the one you left at the Columbus Hotel, which you said you hated." Ethan held up a finger. "Reason number one is that you suddenly decided you don't like me and my house is too messy to bother with cleaning, so you chose to leave behind my back rather than having to face me and possibly being forced into admitting such awkward sentiments."

"Ethan!" Jeanne stared at him. How had he ever come up with such an idea as that?

Ethan added a second finger to the first. "Reason number two is that you've been holding out on me for all these weeks, and in fact you loved working at the Columbus Hotel and have been dying to get back to work emptying chamber pots, washing mounds of dishes, and serving ungrateful customers who sometimes step into your path and cause you to spill your trays of food, then point fingers at you and blame you for causing the disaster they brought on themselves."

"Ethan!" she said again.

He looked up, his eyebrows raised. "What, are neither of those the reason you left?"

"Of course not. That's ridiculous."

Ethan gave her what almost looked like a smirk. "Good. I was hoping it would be reason number three." He held up a third finger. "So if you don't dislike me and my messy house or wish to go back to serving ungrateful customers at a place like the Columbus Hotel, then it must be that you fell in love with me and didn't want to stay for fear that I would guess it."

Jeanne felt the blood drain from her face. How had he guessed? Was she really that obvious? She felt sure her mortification could go no deeper.

Ethan stepped even closer until he was standing right at the wheel, his head tilted back to look up at her. The teasing on his face was gone, and in its place was something softer. "Jeanne, I could have missed my guess and that isn't how you feel about me—but I hope it is. You see, I want to make a new kind of bargain."

Jeanne stared at a button on his shirt. "A—a bargain?"

"Mm, hmm. You'll want to give it some heavy thought, because the bargain I have in mind is going to last a lifetime." He paused. "*Both* our lifetimes."

Jeanne felt sure her heart must be about to pound through her chest. "What did you have in mind?"

"I want you to get down from that wagon. It's giving my neck a crick to look up at you."

"What?" Jeanne looked from him to Ephraim. Ephraim grinned and waved for her to get down.

She didn't have much choice. Ephraim didn't seem inclined to whip the team away from Ethan and his searching gaze, and even if he did, Jeanne knew Ethan would only come after her again.

Sliding off her seat, she climbed down from the wagon. She didn't want to face Ethan, but he placed a hand on her shoulder and turned her around to face him. "Look at me, Jeanne."

She risked a peek at his face. He didn't look angry. Nor did he seem upset. She really couldn't tell what he was feeling.

"I'm afraid this is going to be a rather one-sided bargain, but you'll have a few perks. You'll have a roof over your head, food on the table, and a family who loves you. And for me, the benefits would be that my little girl would have a mother, my house would have a woman in control of it again, and I would get to spend the rest of my life with the woman I love."

Jeanne drew in a sharp breath, but before she could say even a word, Ethan dropped to one knee in front of her. "Please, Jeanne—I'm asking you to marry me. I didn't want you in my life at first, but I can't imagine it without you now. That was why I asked if you would let me hire you. It was never about the job—it was always about *you*. I couldn't let you leave, and I thought I would give us more time to get to know each other, to do a real courtship. But I think that after all we've been through in the past weeks, we know each other better than we would have through any normal courtship. I love you, and I want you to be my wife—"

Jeanne covered her face with her hands, sobs shaking her shoulders. All this time, all this heartache she had put herself through—and he had been *trying* to woo her?

"Jeanne?" She could hear the worry that laced his voice. "Was I wrong to guess that you love me?"

She shook her head, trying to swallow back her tears. "No—I just never thought you would—care about me like that."

"Well, then you'd better believe it." He reached up and pulled her hands away from her face. "I love you, Jeanne McAllister—and I'll tell you as many times as I need to until you believe it."

Jeanne looked into his eyes and saw all the evidence she needed. He really *was* serious.

"Take off your ring," Ethan whispered, and Jeanne pulled her gaze away from his to look down at the ring Irving had given her at their wedding. Why she still wore it she didn't know—but the time had come for her to lay the past aside. And gladly too.

She slid it from her finger, and taking her other hand in his, Ethan slid a different ring onto her hand. Jeanne couldn't help but gasp. It was beautiful, with a delicately engraved gold band and a diamond mounted in the center.

She lifted her eyes to his. "Where did you get this?"

He smiled. "It was my grandmother's. After Grandpa Becker passed away, I inherited it, along with a few of his other special things—my siblings said it was because I was his favorite. Anyhow, Mamie always liked brand-new things, so I tucked the ring away and almost forgot about it. I remembered it a couple weeks ago, and I've been carrying it in my pocket since then. I knew the perfect moment to propose to you was going to come eventually, and I didn't want to be caught unprepared."

"I'll treasure it." Just as she would treasure the man who had given it to her. "It's a perfect fit."

"I'm glad." Ethan looked down at her hand. "My grandparents had a marriage I always admired, and in some ways that ring seems symbolic of it. Neither you nor I have had a happy past, but I'm convinced that God is fully able to restore those years to us. His way is always perfect, isn't it?"

"Always," Jeanne whispered.

From the wagon Ephraim began to whistle, reminding them that he was still there and waiting to get on his way to Columbus. But obviously he had been eavesdropping, because the tune he whistled was Wagner's "Bridal Chorus."

Ethan and Jeanne exchanged a glance.

"I hope you didn't want to keep our engagement a secret, because the news will be out as soon as he gets back to Osceola," Jeanne said under her breath.

"I'm afraid it's already out. Sadie wouldn't let me get away without my answering some questions, and I'm pretty sure she's sitting at home planning our wedding for us right now."

Jeanne couldn't help but laugh. "I'm glad to let her have the fun of that."

"I don't mind either, as long as she lets me make the decision on what we'll have for the meal after the wedding."

Jeanne raised her eyebrows. "And what would that be?"

Ethan grinned. "Roast beef dinner."

EPILOGUE

May 8, 1878

Humming the hymn "Blessed Assurance," Jeanne pinned both sides of the diaper into place, then pulled the long-skirted baby dress down over her son's legs.

"You just get bigger every day, don't you?" she crooned, picking him up and lifting him to her shoulder. He set right to work sucking her shoulder, and she chuckled. He would be ready to eat before too long.

The ring on her finger caught in the sunlight, and Jeanne found herself looking at it. Ethan had been right when he said that God's way is always perfect. Being married to Ethan had turned out to be every bit as wonderful as she had imagined, and she couldn't imagine her life without him, Vivian, and now baby Eli.

Not that they hadn't had their struggles. Even though Ethan had told her he was trusting God to care for her and the unborn baby, she had seen the fear that sometimes crept into his eyes. He had been far more frightened than her when she went into labor, and only Doc Stoning's calm and no-nonsense attitude had kept the birth smooth.

And it *had* been smooth. Doc Stoning said Eli's birth had been one of the easiest he had attended. Jeanne had been tempted to argue with him about using the word *easy*, but Doc had been smart and distracted her with her new son before she could raise much of a fuss

Jeanne patted Eli's back and smiled. Ethan had teased that they ought to name him "Bargain" in memory of the past year, but Jeanne talked him out of that. Instead, they named him after Ethan's Grandpa Becker, and Jeanne felt the name suited him just fine.

"Mama?" Vivian appeared in the parlor doorway, one hand rubbing at her sleep-filled eyes and the other clutching her rag doll.

"Come here, Vivian." Jeanne sat down in the rocker and patted her lap.

Vivian scrambled up, then leaned back against Jeanne and grinned at her brother. Eli stared back at her, and as he gave one hand a little wave, Vivian giggled.

Jeanne heard footsteps on the porch, and she smiled. "Sounds like your papa."

"Papa?" Vivian wiggled down again, eager as ever to run to meet Ethan.

The door opened, and as Ethan called her name, Jeanne said, "In the parlor."

His footsteps came her way and he filled the doorway. "Guess who I found in town today."

"Who?" Jeanne sat up straighter and watched as Ethan moved aside to allow Judge Pratt and Sheriff Calaman in.

"Hello, Mrs. Becker," Judge Pratt said, his voice loud enough that Eli startled and let out a whimper. "Calaman and I heard about the new arrival and figured that since neither of us were able to attend the wedding last summer, we would come visit and see how Ethan was getting along now that he's got a new son."

"Why, how good to see both of you again!" And Jeanne meant it, even if there had been a time when she thought the two men were bent on ruining her life.

Judge Pratt turned to Ethan. "I must say, you look to be doing well. I guess my prescription was what you needed all along, wasn't it?" He nudged Sheriff Calaman, and Calaman frowned.

"Now, Pratt, your idea may have worked out all right, but keep in mind that mine may have too if I'd only been given a chance to try it. Moving him away from Osceola probably would have worked equally well."

"I'm glad that wasn't necessary." Ethan winked at Jeanne and moved to stand beside her rocker. "Nothing could be more perfect than having Jeanne in my life."

Judge Pratt's chest began to puff, but Calaman said, "And keep in mind, Pratt, that you were just as shocked as anyone when you heard that Ethan was marrying Jeanne. This was *not* entirely your doing."

Pratt's eyes narrowed. "But it wouldn't have come about if I hadn't sent her to him."

"But you *thought* she would merely open his eyes to other women."

"And it did. It opened his eyes to *her.*"

"Now, Pratt—"

"No, Calaman—you listen to me—"

Ethan leaned closer to Jeanne and whispered, "Now I know why going to Columbus always makes me so exhausted. It's because I have to put up with these two."

"I'm sorry for you," Jeanne whispered, fighting back a giggle.

Ethan angled his shoulders to block out Pratt and Calaman's bickering and leaned in to steal a kiss from her. "They'll argue about this for the rest of their lives, but I'll always be grateful to them. Regardless of what they say, they never would have foreseen this coming, but they still pushed you into my life, and for that I'll gladly put up with their arguing."

Jeanne closed her eyes as he kissed her one last time and smiled. All of them had been acting blindly except for God, who had been in control the whole time. And He had created a perfect answer to all their needs.

Note to the Reader

A Bargain to Keep is a story that launches off a dream many years in the making, a series set in 1800s Osceola. I'll admit that I'm hopelessly biased to the Osceola area—it was the town I grew up near and it has shaped my family's past for generations.

My idea for a series featuring the Osceola area came a few years ago, but I think the first seeds were planted years before when I stumbled across the amazing scrapbook and picture collection in my great-grandma's basement. There were pictures of the house I grew up in as it was constructed during 1920, glimpses of the everyday life that shaped my great-great-grandparents, and stories and genealogies my great-grandma had preserved with pain-staking detail. *That* was the moment when appreciation for my ancestors and my past came flooding in on me. It opened my eyes to the fingerprints of years gone by that still lingered on my family's farm, and it drove me to learn even more about the past.

This particular story underwent a drastic series of changes before it emerged as it is now. At one point, I was about to give up on it as hopeless. I had already written the whole story, but it was so filled with tragedy that it didn't seem to fit with the rest of the series.

The book had to be rewritten, but I was clean out of ideas—until I brought the plot to my sister. We tossed ideas around as we lay in our beds with the lights out, transforming Jeanne and Ethan into the people they are now, and hitting the "flash of fire" that I always need to bring my stories to life. For this book, that "fire" was the very first chapter—the scene where Jeanne hit Ethan with her platter of roast beef dinner. We laughed to the point of tears over it, I was energized, and I tackled the story the very next day.

On this round, I knew the story was going to work. I had it finished in less than two months, gave it a light polish, and sent it off to my publisher. And to bring the story to "the end," now the book rests completed in your hands.

If you loved this book and want to hear more about the characters, visit my website at **www.alenamentink.com** and sign up for my newsletter to get an extra story about Ephraim and Sadie. To find discussion questions, click on the bonus feature's tab on my website. And the most important thing you could do to promote this book is to leave a review on whichever site you bought it through. Reviews are so important for encouraging others to read this book, and I would consider it a personal favor if you would leave one.

While the author is the one who dreams up the story and writes it alone, there are others in the background who play an important role in turning a manuscript from a pile of marked up pages into a beautiful book.

To show my gratitude to just a few of the people who invested into this book, thank you to Uncle Steve for borrowing the "Osceola book" to me. Thank you to the Osceola Library—I just love the old stacks of books. You are always my number one go-to for research.

Thank you to Electric Moon Publishing. It's been a pleasure to work with you again, and special thanks to Laree for helping me work through the complications that always try to step in the way of forward progress.

Thanks to my family—you always support me and laugh at all the right places in my stories. And Kailey—what can I say? You helped me tear into the very threads of this story and completely overhaul it. Plus, you patiently listened to all my author woes as we sorted laundry, did dishes, and took walks that were supposed to be a step away from business. It probably bored you to tears sometimes, but you didn't complain.

And lastly, to all of the readers who have been patiently waiting for this book, thank you. I appreciate each and every one of you. Whenever I wonder why I bother writing books, I think of your faces and sweet words of encouragement. Your enthusiasm keeps me pushing the keys on the keyboard.

ABOUT THE AUTHOR

ALENA MENTINK is a Nebraska author who enjoys mixing history with fictional characters to create a story for God's glory. When she isn't busy writing, Alena can usually be found somewhere around her family's farm outside of Stromsburg where she lives with her parents and seven siblings.

You may also like . . .

SETTLE MY HEART – Coming west, Brittany had no expectations of dealing with a growly employer, rivaling cowboys, or an unwanted suitor. Despite the hardships, she finds that Wyoming Territory has some redeeming qualities, among them her brother's friend Nathan. But the past still hovers close to the surface and could be the wedge that threatens to keep them apart . . .

www.alenamentink.com

Learn more at

www.alenamentink.com

www.ingramcontent.com/pod-product-compliance
Lightning Source LLC
Chambersburg PA
CBHW051955170626
46808CB00007B/2630